lolly

Kate Petty is the author of many books for children – pop-up books and non-fiction as well as stories. She lives in London with her husband. They have a son and a daughter.

Holly

KATE PETTY

Dolphin Paperbacks

These books are for Rachel, who approved

First published in Great Britain in 2000
as a Dolphin paperback
by Orion Children's Books
a division of the Orion Publishing Group Ltd
Orion House
5 Upper St Martin's Lane
London WC2H 9EA

A catalogue record for this book is available from the British Library

Typeset at The Spartan Press Ltd,
Lymington, Hants
Printed in Great Britain by
Clays Ltd, St Ives plc

ISBN 1 85881 800 1

One

I had to ring my friend Josie straight away when I got home from Barbados. She was never in, of course. I left loads of messages for her, ordering her to call me back just as soon as she could. The summer holidays were half over and I was desperate for us to do what Maddy and *her* friends had done, before it was too late.

I decided to ask the other two, Alex and Zoe, over for the night anyway. I'd almost given up on Josie when she eventually rang me back.

'Yo Holly – it'th Jothie!' She sounded most peculiar.

'Josie?'

'The thame. Don't laugh, Holly. I'm in agony. I've just got a brathe.'

'A what?'

'A *brathe*!'

'Bad luck. Does all your food get stuck in it?'

'I don't know,' she wailed. 'I've only had it for two dayth, and it thtill hurtth.'

'So how do you manage to play the clarinet?' Josie had already spent ten days this holiday tooting her little heart out on a music course.

'I don't. Thatth why I had to wait until the muthic courthe wath out of the way. I won't be able to play again for a year. Anyway – why were you so botthy about me ringing you? I'm not tho thure I want to hear about your amathingly ecthotic time in Barbadoth now.'

'You don't have any choice. But listen, this is why I've been trying to get hold of you. When I was in Barbados I met this girl called Maddy, and she knows Hannah Gross from your music course, and they did this cool thing where they all agreed to have a holiday romance and meet up afterwards to report. No cheating. I wanted to catch you before you went to Cornwall so we can do the same. Come over tomorrow night? The others are. We can plan it then.'

'Romanthe? With thith thing in my mouth? You mutht be joking! But I'll come anyway. I do want to hear about Barbadoth really. And the entire cricket team.'

(I'd better explain. The holiday in Barbados was with my dad and the under-16s cricket team from the school where he teaches. Mum went as nurse and us daughters went free. Absolutely a one-off, you understand – we don't usually go further than Wales.)

Josie's speech was vastly improved by the time they all came over. I think she was doing it a bit for effect before, but she said the brace was much less painful. Not pleasant. Glad I don't have to have one. She arrived before Zoe and Alex to help me organise the pizzas – she said it was the first time she'd felt like eating anything. I think she'd even lost weight, and she was fairly thin to start off with. Josie's got long, fairish hair and blue eyes – and a brace. She's always had sticking-out teeth, but I think she'll be really pretty once they're straightened out.

I was allowed to have the front room for the sleepover. My bedroom's a box room over the front door and barely big enough for me, let alone four of us! I used to share bunk beds with my younger sister, Abby. She still has the bunks and the big room to go with them but I was allowed to decorate my little room exactly as I wanted – fake fur cushion covers, fairy lights from IKEA and all my own posters. It's fab. My parents say we'll never be able to afford a mansion, but I love our house and I wouldn't want to move, even if it was to somewhere bigger.

Alex lives in our road. She's got loads of brothers. They're all energetic and sporty, and so's her Dad, but her mum's a bit of a doormat. Probably has to be, running around after that lot. Alex used to be a complete tomboy – it took her forever to get round to wearing a bra – but though she's tall and skinny with short hair and freckles she's looking more like a girl these days. She's got a wicked sense of humour too. Everybody laughs a lot when Alex is around. She's one of those people who can remember jokes and do impressions. She turned up in her 'sweats' as she calls them, from playing tennis. 'Like the metal, Josie,' she said. 'Gives a whole new meaning to the "flashing smile" '. So of course, Josie flashed her metal smile. Alex handed over a Tesco bag with four cans of shandy. She'd somehow persuaded her dad to buy it for us. She's got him wrapped round her little finger.

Between us we hauled down mattresses and campbeds and duvets and sleeping bags. My little sister seems to spend half the holidays away at sleepovers, so we could have had her room, but there isn't a TV or video in there. Anyway, it was cool transforming the front room. Basically we just made a big nest in front of the TV and cleared a space on the coffee table for food and drink.

Zoe turned up just as we'd finished getting the room ready. Alex, Josie and me have been together since the infants, and we were a threesome for ages. Zoe moved in a bit later. Alex knew her already because the twins are friends with Zoe's younger brother – you know how it is. The four of us are pretty close these days, especially in the holidays (not least because Josie's parents took her away from our school after the first year). But this summer I'd been in Barbados, Zoe had been to Italy and Josie had been on the music course, so there was a whole load of catching up to do.

See Zoe and you'd assume she was a model or a pop star – she's that gorgeous. In fact she can't sing to save her life (she is brilliant at acting though). But underneath that fabulously beautiful exterior is a keen, keen brain. She took up debating last term and she's brilliant at that too. Demolishes the opposition – usually male, usually making the assumption that she's an airhead – with a few well chosen incisive comments. Makes your hair stand on end. Honestly, she even makes 'This House believes bloodsports should be abolished' – or whatever – exciting!

We've got our priorities right, so we concentrated on eating our pizzas before talking, but once we'd got started the others made me tell them about Barbados and the girl I'd met there – Maddy. And of course, the boy I'd met there, too – Jonty Hayter.

'So you've already had one romance!' said Zoe. 'That's not fair! Are you expecting to have another one?'

'*I* thertainly won't,' said Josie, 'me and my metal mouth.'

'I don't think I do romance, do I?' said Alex.

'Shut up! Shut up! *Shut up!*' I yelled. 'You mean lot. I'm not going to talk about it until later, when you're prepared to hear me out. OK? Now, be quiet. Watch the video.' I pointed the remote at the TV and all noise subsided as the opening credits for *Titanic* rolled.

In fact we didn't discuss the romance plan again until *Titanic* was over and we'd all cried buckets and were snuggled up in our makeshift beds. Josie had snitched more than her fair share of duvet and Alex was mucking about and making more jokes than usual at my expense so I thought it was time for a bit of control here. (It's not my fault I'm a teacher's daughter.)

'OK!' I shouted. 'Now I'm going to tell you my plan, whether you like it or not.'

'I like it already!' said Alex in a 'Goodness Gracious Me' voice, while Josie took the opportunity to haul the duvet over to her side again. I chose to ignore them both.

'These four girls, right? – Maddy, Hannah – from Josie's music course, and two others, all had a sleepover at the beginning of the holidays. *Where* they agreed to have holiday romances and report back on them at the end of the holidays. Well, I know for a fact that Maddy had a romance—'

'Ha! So did Hannah!' said Josie, 'eventually, but I didn't know it wath to order. And it nearly didn't happen . . .'

'Well, having to report back obviously focused the brain,' I carried on. '*Anyway* . . . I met Jonty and he was brilliant and I'm madly in love with him—'

'I'm glad for you, Holly,' said Alex – her American agony-aunt voice this time.

'*Anyway* – ' I said again, 'I'm going to stay with his family for a week. What I haven't told you is that the Hayters are, like, *mega*-rich. They're blue-blooded aristos who go back to the Domesday Book with a vast estate in Warwickshire and a house in Chelsea and they go huntin' and shootin' and have balls and stuff – and

Mum is worried that we'll find we don't have anything in common.'

'She might have a point there,' said Zoe, popping her eyes and suppressing a smile.

'Maybe she does, but I think love should *triumph* over our differences, don't you? Jonty's so cute – he doesn't care that I'm not rich!'

'Of course not,' said Alex. 'He just loves you for your raven tresses, your shining eyes, your bushy tail and your adorable personality.'

'Wow. A ball,' said Josie wistfully. 'Lucky you.'

'Thank you. Exactly.' I wished they'd all shut up and listen. 'So, that's *my* holiday romance, and I'll tell you all how I got on the last weekend before term starts – and we all go into year ten. My God – soon we'll all be *fifteen*! Maddy's fifteen next month.'

'So am I,' said Zoe. 'OK. My problem is, I don't plan to do anything much for the next couple of weeks. I didn't exactly find romance in Tuscany with my family – mind you, everyone there was English or American, and *white!*' she said with a laugh. 'Even after three weeks! Except for me and my brother. And Mum of course. Back to the point, girl – so what chance do I have back here? I might just go on this Community Theatre thing with Tark. We'll see. No promises. But I'll *try*, Holly, I'll *try*!'

Alex was still laughing. 'Tennis tournament – county number. Fit young men by the score, but interested in *me*? I think not. The women maybe.' We looked at her quizzically. She shrank. 'Tennis, you know!'

'Phew,' said Josie. 'I thought maybe there was something you weren't telling us!'

'Maybe there is,' said Alex. 'But romance I will seek. With a fit young man. And I will report back, on love games, lost balls and every other corny tennis pun you can think of. Happy?'

I considered. 'I suppose it doesn't *have* to be with a member of the opposite sex . . .' I said cautiously.

'Per-lease!' said Josie. 'Anyway, you can all hear about my holiday now, because mine is actually quite exciting.'

'Oh good,' said Alex. Zoe gave me a quick sympathetic smile.

'The music course was boring,' said Josie. 'The boys were pathetic. Well, Hannah's one was OK. And there were one or two others. I suppose.'

'But none of them fancied you. Carry on,' said Alex.

'I couldn't care less,' said Josie, slightly wounded, 'because we're off to our cottage in Cornwall as usual, and there are squillions—'

'Thkwillionth?' said Alex.

'A great number – ' said Josie carefully, '– of gorgeous guys down there. And there is one I have had my eye on for some time now and I shall force him to lock braces with me before the holiday is over and report back.'

'Does he wear a brace too?' I asked. It seemed unlikely.

'He might do,' said Josie. 'And if he doesn't, I might have to look for someone who does. OK? Have I passed?'

'Excellent!' Zoe clapped. 'I think we've done very well, don't you Holly? And now I want to watch something x-rated on TV and drink alcohol – if it's all the same with you guys.'

'I can't find him anywhere.' Dad was peering through his reading glasses at the small print of *Burke's Peerage*. 'Perhaps he's an impostor.'

'I doubt it,' said Mum, switching off the TV. 'Here, let me look. My eyesight's better for the wee type.' (Needless to say, Mum's Scottish.)

'No,' said Dad. 'I can see all right. There are Hayters listed here, but none called Brian and none in Warwickshire.'

'Tell you what,' said Mum. 'It's probably the reverse. They're probably posher. I bet they're double-barrelled. Are you sure they're not double-barrelled dear?' She turned to me.

'Don't think so.' I was beginning to get fed up with their sudden interest in Jonty's family. They said it was because they weren't just going to let me go off and stay with him without checking them out, but they were sniggering a bit too much and I didn't like it.

Abby piped up from where she was reading in the corner with the cat on her lap. 'Jonty's real name is Jonathan James Rye Clermont-Hayter,' she said in a sing-song voice. 'He told me.'

We all looked at her in surprise. 'It's more than he told me!' I said.

'Too busy snogging you,' said Abby, going back to her book.

'That's enough of that, young lady,' said Mum. 'And it's high time you were in bed, Abby. You hardly had any sleep at your so-called sleepover. Run along and get into your pyjamas.'

'Found him!' said Dad loudly. 'Well, well, well, my little Holly. It looks as if you're going to be staying with the nobs.'

'Beg pardon, Dad?'

'The gentry, my dear. I've found them. Our Brian and Gina are Sir Brian and Lady Clermont-Hayter. And no doubt, young Jonty, when his father dies, will inherit the title. What do you think of that? You'd better learn to curtsey!'

I told them it didn't affect me either way and that I was going to bed too. Between you and me, all this stuff about the gentry was actually making me nervous. All Dad's boys are well off, they have to be to afford the fees. Mostly they're like other people – some nice and some not, but I do sometimes resent their attitudes. It's not just envy. Mum and Dad are solid Labour voters, and basically disapprove of all right-wing sentiments, so of course it's rubbed off on me. But I didn't want to be reminded of it as far as Jonty was concerned. Right then I wanted only the company of my diary and Jonty's letters. He'd started when I left him behind in Barbados and somehow we'd carried on communicating by post – well, a couple of letters either way anyway. That was how we'd fixed up my visit. We'd put some really lovey-dovey stuff in the letters, quite embarrassing really, so I'd reached a point where I would actually have felt quite shy talking to him on the phone.

I got ready for bed and curled up under my duvet. I keep my diary right in my bed – I reckon Mum and Abby won't stoop to looking for it there. I hauled it up. It's one of those hardbacked exercise books you buy in Smiths. I write in it every day and decorate the pages with different coloured pens and bits cut out of magazines. You know the sort of thing. I take a lot of pride in it, but it is *strictly* for myself. I stick letters and photos in there too – it's got rather fat and difficult to close since Barbados.

I turned back to the day I first saw Jonty in Barbados. I'd been on the beach with the boys from Dad's school, little sister Abby and some of the other staff daughters. The boys were playing an impromptu ball game half in the water and half out of it and we girls were sunbathing at the top of the beach. I'd seen a lone boy – who wasn't one of ours, though he looked about the same age – hanging round the ball game as if he wanted to join in. And you know how boys are – it wasn't long before he was part of the game.

Barbados
Met a boy today – not from Beale College. I watched him join in our boys' beach game and then he came back up the beach with them. He didn't talk to me – I just watched him. He's called Jonty and he's got a nice smily face – not particularly goodlooking, just nice. Tanned, like everybody. He's got ordinary brownish wavy floppy hair that gets in his eyes (I'm not sure what colour they are yet.) He's quite tall and skinny but what I noticed most was the way he moves. Kind of elegant. When he runs he sort of flickers. He got pally with the lads very quickly. I could hear him making them laugh. He's got rather a posh accent, but then so have most of Dad's boys, and a nice croaky sort of voice. I hope I see him again tomorrow.

Of course I did see him quite a lot after that. He was staying in one of the ultra-smart hotels, but I heard him saying he'd been there so much he was bored with it. We should be so lucky! I didn't talk to him, but I did like watching him. It wasn't that he was particularly handsome or anything, just very confident and happy with himself. Some days later he appeared with the most gorgeous looking bloke I've ever seen – American and way out of my league, not least because he was a couple of years older than our boys. And then the hunky guy's younger sister came along and joined up with us girls. That was Linden. Her brother was called Red and they turned out to be the kids of Oliver O'Neill (only *the* most famous film director in the world). And *then*, of course, I met Maddy; not American, not rich, just amazingly beautiful – and well, the rest of that is Maddy's story. But it was because of Maddy, and that first barbecue, that I got to know Jonty and his family.

It still seems like a dream really. I fell completely in love with Jonty out there. His sister Dilly is nice too, but the oldest one, Flavia, is ghastly. So when I got the letter from Jonty asking me to come and stay with his family in the country, my pleasure wasn't completely undiluted.

Holly, my gorgeous Holly, PLEASE come and stay down here with me. I want to come up to London but the parents think I'm too young to be in Chelsea on my own. Unlike Flavia who is there most of the time. But Dilly's going off on some horse thing so they're happy for you to come and stay for the week while she's away. I don't quite see the connection – there are ten million rooms here – but hey, who am I to complain? There ain't much going on down here in the country, but that won't matter if we can only be together. I miss you heaps. Please say you'll come,
Jont xxxxxxx

So I'm going. Jonty's mum rang my mum to say it was all OK. My mum asked what I should bring and his mum just said, 'Oh, the usual things. Riding gear and a tennis racquet might be a good idea. And I think someone's having a do, so perhaps a fancy frock to be on the safe side.'

That last item was what blew Mum apart. 'Oxfam shop,' she said. 'We might find something in one of the upmarket ones. Or something I can cut up and turn into a ball gown.' No trips to Monsoon for me then. Needless to say, we traipsed round every charity shop and secondhand shop in Hampstead and even Camden, but we didn't find anything. We looked at material in John Lewis – *gorgeous* silks and velvets – and paper patterns, but nothing seemed right, let alone the right price. Then Mum remembered that my cousin Daisy had been to a May Ball earlier in the year, so she rang Daisy's mum to see if I could borrow Daisy's dress. Daisy's family is chaos, so although they said yes, of course, no one could lay their hands on the dress at that precise moment. In the end they agreed to post it to me at Jonty's house. So that was that little problem solved.

We looked up trains and coaches (cheaper), but then Jonty's mum rang again to say that Flavia was driving up from town on that day, so why not have a lift from Chelsea?

Why not indeed.

The night before I was due to go I rang Maddy. 'I'll come over,' she said.

'How?' I said.

'Bus,' said Maddy. She's so much more streetwise than me. I wouldn't want to cross our bit of London on public transport on my own, even if my parents would let me, but she couldn't care less. She got here in just over an hour as well. She went through my case item by item. 'Bikini, good. Jeans for riding, plus – ooh, proper riding boots!'

'Cousin Daisy's cast-offs.'

'Tennis racquet. Whites. Doing well, Holly. So where's the ballgown?'

'Funny you should mention that.'

'Well, you remember me in Barbados. I had to borrow one. And Dilly and Flavia had all the kit. Flavia wore the crown jewels, remember?'

'I wasn't there, Maddy. Though of course I heard about it.'

'Beware the fabulously rich, my dear. Remember, we're normal. They're not.'

'Thanks for those words of advice, Maddy. Anyway, Cousin Daisy is coming to the rescue again with the ballgown.'

'Let's see it.'

'They're posting it straight to Jonty's, but Daisy wore it to a May Ball this year and she's got good taste. It'll be fine.'

'Well, let's hope so!'

It was hot in the car. London was full of tourists and cyclists. I was jittery. Abby was bored. Mum was driving and Dad was getting cross with her. It wasn't a great start. We got lost in the little streets and one-way systems in Chelsea, though Abby cheered up because there were lots of pedigree dogs to point out. We got there half an hour late. Hot and bothered, and wishing I hadn't forgotten my sunglasses, I went up the twee (pretty, really) garden path with my suitcase and pressed the doorbell. Mum and Dad and Abby stood behind me like dorks. Nothing happened. I pressed again. After an age I could hear someone in flip-flops approaching the front door. It opened and there was Flavia looking pink in a bikini with shades pushed on to her head. She eyed us suspiciously. 'Yah?'

'Hi Flavia.' She looked nonplussed. An extremely short man came down the corridor behind her. I recognised Flavia's jockey boyfriend.

'Problem, Flaves?'

'It's the kid Jonty met on holiday. Don't know why she's here.'

'It's me, Holly, Flavia. I thought – Your mother said—'

Dad stepped forward. 'Flavia, your mother led us to believe you were driving home today and that Holly could have a lift. Is that still all right?'

'Suppose so.' She looked at us. I felt somewhat awkward, to put it mildly.

But there was no way I was going home again. I took a deep breath. ' 'Bye Mum, Dad, Abby. I'll watch telly while Flavia gets ready. I don't mind waiting.' I waved back at them and simply pushed my way into the bijou residence with my case.

It got worse. Flavia virtually *ignored* me for the next couple of hours. I sat in front of the television in the dark front room, torturing myself with the worry that Jonty would act all snooty like his sister once he was on his home ground too, until I just had to come out and go to the loo. I ventured out into the garden where Flavia and her boyfriend were *having lunch* (without offering me any)! She didn't bat an eyelid – simply told me where the loo was. After about another hour there was a ring at the doorbell followed by shrieks and giggles from two other girls. I decided to go and see what was happening. One girl was about my age and the other about eighteen, like Flavia. They were both tall and blonde and skinny and both were festooned with about ten designer carrier bags each. Major clothes shopping had taken place.

'Got room for Tamara?' asked the older one. 'She's bought even more than I have but she doesn't take up much space.' She laughed unkindly.

'Suppose so,' said Flavia – her usual answer.

I decided to remind her of my presence. 'When are we going, Flavia?'

'Do we know you?' asked the older one.

'Friend of Jont's,' said Flavia in reply. 'Ma asked me to give her a lift.'

'Oh.'

'I don't think it's fair if I have to go on the train,' said the one called Tamara in a whiny voice. 'I think you should, Beatrice. You're older.'

The jockey appeared at Flavia's elbow. 'Problem, Flaves?'

'Yah,' said Flavia. 'We've got to get four people into my car.'

'That's not a problem is it?' said the jockey.

'It is with all these bags,' said Beatrice.

I couldn't stand it any longer. 'For heaven's sake!' I said. 'It must be a tiny car if it can't fit four people!'

'But what about the bags?' said Tamara. She really was stick thin, and her mouth hung open all the time.

The jockey actually came to my rescue. 'Go and dress, Dumpling,' he said to Flavia. 'I'll put these togs in the boot for you and then you can all fit in.'

'As long as you're careful!' said Beatrice imperiously.

Needless to say, everything fitted in. Apart from me – socially, that is. Flavia never thought to explain that I'd simply arrived earlier than she was expecting and that we were waiting for her friends to arrive before setting off. Honestly, the arrogance of the girl! How could my lovely Jonty have such a nasty sister?

Beatrice sat in the front with Flavia. I sat in the back with Tamara, who ignored me. Flavia drove at great speed. She obviously felt she owned the motorway – like everything else. I nodded off but was woken by gales of uproarious laughter as we swept into the gravel drive of a vast mansion.

'Jonty's got a *girlfriend*?' snorted Beatrice. 'I don't believe it!'

'I know, it is unbelievable, isn't it?' *Thank you, Flavia.*

'Whatever sort of girl could fancy that spotty little twerp?' said Beatrice, climbing out of the car. 'She must be frightfully dim, or short-sighted or something!'

The other two followed her. Flavia opened the boot and handed them all the ten billion bags. More giggles and sniggers. 'Sssh,' said Flavia, not realising that I'd heard it all. 'You've just been sharing a car with her!' As she waved them off amidst more guffaws, I saw Tamara glowering back at me. Flavia got into the car and roared away down the gravel drive at a hundred miles an hour.

Twenty minutes later we turned off the road past a lodge and through an ornate stone gateway. We drove for nearly a mile down an avenue of chestnut trees. There were fields beyond the chestnut trees. Some of them contained horses. At last we drove over a little bridge and rounded a bend. Before me was a stately pile, Jonty's home. And running to meet us were three droopy little spaniels – and Jonty.

Boy was I glad to see him.

Three

I couldn't get out of that car fast enough. I flung myself enthusiastically into Jonty's arms, and we clung on to each other for what seemed like ages. He buried his face in my hair. 'Oh Holly! You just – smell wonderful,' he said, and then stood back, abashed.

'You don't smell so bad yourself,' I quipped, and then felt silly. We both looked down at our shoes for a moment while the dogs sniffed around us excitedly.

Embarrassed, he introduced the dogs. 'Meet Flopsy, Mopsy and Popsy,' he said. 'King Charleses. Popsy's the boy and I'm afraid he farts rather a lot.' There was no answer to that. 'Let's get your stuff then,' said Jonty, quite formally, pleased to have something to do. He grabbed my hand and we scrunched over the drive to Flavia's car. She'd left all the car doors open but she hadn't bothered to wait. He gallantly led the way into the house carrying my case, prattling away about all the things he had planned for us to do. I followed him with my tennis racquet, not taking in anything he was saying. He looked slightly different from my memory of him and I couldn't think why. Then I realised he'd had a haircut – some of his floppy wavy fringe had gone. It made him look both older and younger, if that's possible. The spaniels wove in and out, doing their best to trip us up.

The low evening sun had been dazzling, so it took a while for my eyes to adjust to the darkness of the hall once we'd gone in through the porticoed doors, the dogs skittering along after us. I don't know why I had expected anything else, but it was just like something out of *Country Life* (sole reading material at our local vet's surgery). The hall was about the same size as our entire house with a grey stone flagged floor and a polished oak table bearing a beautiful arrangement of pink and white roses and sweet peas. There were dim portraits on the oak panelled walls. Stairs curved up on either side and I looked up to see a balcony above. Downstairs, several doors opened on to corridors that led into the distance. It was unbelievable. Mum had been rather disparaging about the Hayters' taste in Barbados, but this was simply centuries of quality. It smelt of cool stone and beeswax and summer flowers. 'Wow, Jonty. What an amazing house!' (The word 'house' didn't do it justice.)

'Welcome to Clermont Chase,' said Jonty. 'A small place, but my own – at least it will be one day.' He said it with a laugh, but of course it was true. Blimey. I remembered joking with Maddy that I was going to marry Jonty and be frightfully rich. Well, one day *somebody* would.

Gina, Jonty's mum, appeared through one of the doors. She was carrying a clinking glass of gin and tonic. 'Oh hello dear,' she said, not unkindly but vaguely, as if she had forgotten I was coming. 'Show your friend where she'll be sleeping, Jonathan. I think Mrs B. has done the green room, you know – at the back, a couple of doors along from Flavia.' Can you believe it?

'OK,' said Jonty. 'Follow me.' And he lugged my case up one of the staircases. We walked round the balcony to the back of the house and a row of rooms that overlooked the gardens and the ornamental pool. Jonty opened a door – 'Oops, no, that's the yellow room,' and then another, the green room. Fancy not *knowing* all the rooms in your house! But it was fabulous. The full-length windows faced west so the sun slanted in on to the dark, glowing floorboards and the green and red Persian carpet, up over the four-poster bed with a dark green silk awning and bedspread and on to the gleaming surfaces of the oil paintings of various pastoral and hunting (yuk!) scenes. In the corner by the window was a table with another gorgeous flower arrangement – yellow roses this time, with red hot pokers and orange lilies.

'Who does the flowers?' I asked Jonty. 'Is it your mother?'

'Ma? You must be joking! No – it's Jill, Christopher's mum. She likes to practise on the flowers from our gardens.' He opened a door in the wall. 'Here's your bathroom. All mod cons at Clermont Chase.'

After the bedroom it was indeed very modern. Double basin, power shower. Lots of mirrors surrounded by filmstar lights. Fluffy towels. Sea shell full of tiny soaps. No expense spared. 'Who's Christopher?'

We went back into the bedroom. 'You'll meet him tomorrow. He's coming to play tennis with us in the morning. Oldest friend. I've known Christopher since I was two and he was three. Do you want to be left to – er – powder your nose? Wash your hands, that sort of thing?'

I couldn't get used to seeing Jonty embarrassed. 'OK. I'm dying for the loo after that car ride, but I might get lost trying to find you again.'

'I'll meet you in the hall in twenty minutes, and then we'll go for dinner together. OK? Can you find your way down?'

'Hope so,' I said, and I was on my own. After Jonty had gone I sat on the amazing four-poster bed and bounced up and down a few times. I hung my clothes in the wardrobe and laid out my underwear in the paper-lined drawers. I ventured into the wonderful bathroom and could have spent hours playing there. Actually I did have a quick wash before changing into fresh clothes and then went and stood by the open window. The sun was setting over the gardens and the ornamental pond and the woods in the distance. The Forest of Arden perhaps – this was Shakespeare's county after all. I could see walled gardens and greenhouses off to the left and stables off to the right. There were landscaped hills with a glimpse of more water further off and a few small buildings dotted around – summerhouses and follies. I could just hear the sounds of tennis being played but the court was out of sight. I looked at my watch. I still had five minutes. Just time to write my diary. I pulled it out and sat with it in the window seat.

Sunday afternoon
Wow. What am I doing here? Me, Holly Davies at Clermont Chase, home of Sir and Lady Hayter-Clermont?? With a four-poster bed and my own posh bathroom! The journey here was ghastly, but it was worth it in the end. Jonty's got all sorts of things lined up for us to do – mostly riding and playing tennis. That's fine by me, as long as we get time by ourselves to just be. *He's being lovely – not a bit like Flavia. More later. Now I have to go and dine!!!!!!!*

I suppose that after everything I'd seen so far I was expecting us to eat in a great dining hall with butlers and silver and stuff. I was wrong, certainly for tonight. The kitchen at the back of the house was where the Hayters spent most of their time. It was actually quite normal – in a large 'country-style' way, with pine (or oak, probably) units and floral curtains and a big efficient looking cooker as well as an Aga and a microwave, and a vast American fridge. There was a utility room off it (Jonty showed me while he fetched ice for my coke) with an even vaster freezer, washing machines (two) and tumble driers (two).

We sat round the kitchen table, Brian (his dad), Gina (his mum), Flavia, Jonty and me. Apparently Gina hardly ever cooks, preferring to stuff the freezer with food from Marks and Sparks. Her mother never cooked, because there were always staff. Gina told me she was taught domestic science at school but she always found it a 'frightful bore'. Tonight our meal had been left for us by the famous Mrs B., Jonty's one-time nanny but now general housekeeper and mother-figure to the entire family, it seemed. Brian was wildly appreciative. Nursery food has never lost its appeal for him and he tucked in enthusiastically to tomato soup (tinned, I'm sure), baked potatoes and cauliflower cheese followed by apple crumble and cream. 'Mrs B. is a *superb* cook,' he informed me between courses. 'Gina's marvellous in the kitchen too,' he added loyally, 'but Mrs B. always starts with the raw ingredients.' (Whereas Gina starts by opening the packet, I thought to myself.) He dabbed at his mouth with a napkin. 'We're very lucky to have her.'

Flavia, who had been silent up until then, suddenly barked 'Yah?' I realised she'd been palming a cordless digital phone all this time. 'Oh,' she barked again, disappointedly this time, 'It's you. Ma – Cordelia.' She passed the phone across me to Jonty's mother. Cordelia (Dilly – Jonty's nice sister) was passed all round the table and finally to me.

'How's it going, Hol?'

'Dilly! I've only been here an hour.'

'I thought Flavia was driving you up at lunch time.'

I gave Flavia a sidelong glance, turned away from her and lowered my voice. 'Well, that's what I thought, but we gave two girls a lift.'

'Oh God. Beatrice and Tamara I bet. They never come when they say they're going to. Silly tarts, the pair of them. Did they have loads of shopping?'

'Well, yes, they did actually.'

'That's what they do. Shop. Scarcely a neurone between them. Anyway. Don't let them get you down, or my darling sister. I have to go – by the way, have you seen James lately?'

James was one of Dad's boys on the cricket trip. He and Dilly had a bit of a romance in Barbados. 'I have, as it happens. I told him I was coming to stay here and he was very jealous and sends his love.'

'Hmm. Better write to him I suppose. OK, must dash. Byeee!' Phew. Dilly was a breath of normality in this unusual household.

The others were tucking into the apple crumble and cream by then. As I ate mine I looked round the table surreptitiously. Flavia – horsy face and frizzy red hair; Gina, source of the horsy features but goodlooking in a suntanned, leathery sort of way; Brian, balding, but pleasant faced; and my lovely Jonty – also suntanned, light brown, slightly wavy hair and the same crinkly, smily face as his dad, loose limbs akimbo as he sprawled in his hard kitchen chair. Jonty caught my gaze. He scraped his chair back noisily. 'I'm going to show Holly round the estate,' he said, getting to his feet. I stood up too and carried my plate to the sink. 'Don't worry about those, Holly. Mrs B. will see to them in the morning. Come on, let's go.'

I could hear Flavia snorting as we went down the

passage to the back door. 'Practically' (she pronounced it 'praktikleh') 'dark!' she said, as if it mattered to her.

The spectacular sunset was reflected in the ornamental pool as Jonty and I sat down beside it. A small fountain tinkled away in the centre and I could see some huge goldfish darting amongst the water lilies. Jonty put his arm around me and I leant against him. It was strange being out there just with him, and hardly anyone else around. In Barbados he always seemed to be off doing things with his family, just like I was with the cricket team – we were always being pulled in different directions. Now we sat there, gazing at the rippling sunset. I'd been there over an hour and we hadn't even kissed yet. I glanced up at Clermont Chase. 'Look Jonty, the windows are all on fire in the sunset!'

'Aaggh! My butt is on fire!' laughed Jonty (shattering the romantic mood somewhat). He leapt up and ran round like a kid being an aeroplane. I imagined all the frogs on the lilypads plopping straight into the water to escape. But it looked so brilliant I got up and ran around with him, both of us going 'Vmmmmm, vmmmmm, vrrrrrrrrrrrrrrrrrrrrm!' as we went. 'Follow me to the topiary garden!' called Jonty, so I whooshed after him to a lawn surrounded by tall shaped hedges. It was dusk in there, and you could feel the cool air coming up from the grass.

We stopped and stood, feeling the change in the light and the temperature. Then Jonty walked towards me. 'No prying eyes here,' he said as we stood facing one another. He picked up my hand and toyed with my fingers. 'I feel a bit shy, all of a sudden,' he said.

'Me too.' I looked down and my hair fell across my face. It's dark and long and usually I tie it back, but I'd taken out my ponytail when I changed for supper. Jonty reached forward and pushed it back. Cue for a kiss, standing where we were in the twilit gazebo. It was lovely, but strange too, knowing that we had a whole week ahead of us. No one was going to try and separate us.

Total freedom was kind of scary. I think Jonty felt the same way, because before too long he announced that he was getting cold and there was something we could watch on TV, unless I wanted a game of pool in the games room. The *games* room! Or play a computer game, or listen to him on his electric guitar . . . We headed indoors. I could still hear someone playing tennis. 'Jonty, who plays tennis at this time of night?'

'That's probably Christopher and his brother. They can use the court whenever they want. Christopher's got a tournament coming up. You'll see how good he is when we play tomorrow. By the way, Tamara Hilton will make up the four. I haven't seen her for ages, but it means we can play mixed doubles.'

Sunday evening
This is totally amazing – the bed, the room, the house, the grounds, the King Charles spaniels – everything! Jonty is brilliant, really sweet and really shy compared with when we were in Barbados, which is cute (and rather sexy in a way). I wish Dilly was here because she's so normal, but no good wishing. Flavia is a complete witch and the parents are OK but just so different from anyone I know. Tomorrow I get to see Tamara again, yuk, and meet the mysterious tennis player. I'm knackered, so night night diary. More tomorrow.

Four

There's one thing I hate about staying in other people's houses, and that's not knowing what to do first thing in the morning. You wake up and listen to what's going on, and if it's all quiet you stay put. I'm terrified of going downstairs and making the dogs bark or setting off a burglar alarm or catching the dad in his underpants or something. At least I've got my own bathroom and loo – I don't have the problem of bursting in on Brian or Flavia on the toilet. Eugh. So. I listened for a bit and didn't hear anything. Then I thought I might as well get up and have a shower. Didn't think to look at my watch. Had a shower, shaved my legs. Dressed in jeans, then remembered about playing tennis. Put on shorts (khaki as it happens) and a white top and trainers and went to open my curtains and view the estate . . . *Then* I remembered to look for my watch. It had dropped on the floor by the bed. It was half-past ten! So late! How embarrassing!

I shot downstairs, went through a wrong door or two and, after catching up with the dogs, who'd come to sniff me out, finally made it into the kitchen. No one batted an eyelid. Jonty was there, in riding boots. Flavia was there in her dressing gown, hair all over the place, looking more witchy than ever. Gina was just off to the estate office. She said briskly, 'Morning Holly. Help yourself to breakfast because no one else will! Do have fun playing tennis. See you all later!' and whisked off.

Jonty stood up, not quite sure how to greet me at his family breakfast table. I saved him the trouble of hugging/kissing me by sitting down and pouring cereal into the empty bowl that was there. 'Jonty, why didn't you wake me?' I asked.

'I thought you'd probably like a lie-in,' he said. I could see already that Jonty's life was dug in to its own momentum and routines. There was no way my short stay was going to alter years, decades, centuries of life at Clermont Chase.

'Have you been up for ages?'

'I wanted to go out with the horses this morning. There's a new three-year-old our trainer's trying out.'

'Were they the horses I saw in the field by the drive when I arrived?'

Flavia snorted but Jonty cut in. 'Oh no. Those ones are our hunters. This one's a racehorse. He's with the trainer in Lotbourne.'

Flavia had to have her sneer. 'I suppose Bea and I *could* go hacking on the race horses, but I think we'll just stick to dear old Arnold and Sylvester this time.'

She'd lost me there. 'Horses,' said Jonty. 'Schwarze-negger and Stallone. Arnie and Sly. I'm afraid I was allowed to name then when I was about eight.'

'Cretinous, even then,' said Flavia.

'Well *you* named the dogs!' retorted Jonty. 'You can't get much more pathetic than Flopsy, Mopsy and Popsy, can you?' The dogs heard their names and proceeded to shuffle along the floor towards Jonty. A terrible smell emanated from the appropriately named Popsy.

The dogs' attention was diverted by the arrival of Beatrice and Tamara. 'Ciao!' Their voices preceded them from the door at the end of the passage. 'We're here!' (Duh.) Then they appeared in the kitchen – and their appearance was pretty diverting too. They had been dropped off by car, but Beatrice was in riding gear – not that unusual in these parts. Tamara on the other hand was decked out in the total tennis *outfit* – a silky, dazzling white track suit and an expensive-looking designer-label tennis shirt, the latest white trainers and *two* tennis racquets in the double case. She even wore a clip round her waist for tennis balls.

Jonty grinned and caught my eye. 'Say hello to my friend, Jonathan,' said Flavia. 'You remember Beatrice, don't you?' She didn't bother to introduce Tamara, but since the dopey girl was gawping at Jonty anyway, there probably wasn't much point.

'Of course I do,' said Jonty, collecting himself. 'Hi you two! Long time no see!'

Not that Beatrice and Tamara said anything to us of course.

'You've already met Holly, haven't you?' said Jonty. Silence.

'Er, hi,' I said, quietly, on account of feeling invisible.

Flavia stood up and yawned. 'Better dress I suppose. Make some coffee, little brother. Would you like some?' She addressed Beatrice (not me).

'Yah,' said Beatrice.

Jonty's very obliging. He made coffee in a cafetière (I'm not sure that I'd know how to) and dumped it in the middle of the table with some mugs. Then he told Tamara that it was time to meet up with Christopher. 'Are you going to come with us now or follow on when you've had coffee?' He bent under the table to drag out a pair of trainers.

'Don't drink coffee,' was Tamara's only answer. (So rude!)

Jonty was patient. 'So you'll come with Holly and me now?' Completely unselfconsciously he pulled off his riding boots and jeans and put on a manky old pair of shorts and some trainers.

Tamara winced. 'No.'

I wanted to scream, but Jonty's obviously used to people like this. 'See you at the court in about five minutes then?'

'Yah.' Good old Tamara. I'm amazed she and Beatrice and Flavia ever manage to hold proper conversations.

The day had started hazy but it was beginning to heat up as Jonty and I made our way to the tennis court that was hidden round the side of the house behind the rhododendrons. I could hear someone practising a few serves as we approached – I would never have found the court on my own, it was that secluded. Obviously it wasn't a problem with Jonty leading me by the hand. I was beginning to feel curious about Christopher. I imagined he'd look like a famous tennis player – Tim Henman perhaps. And of course he'd be brilliant – I was OK hitting a tennis ball around with Dad and Abby, but suddenly I realised I was rubbish really. Tamara would probably be well coached too. All that gear – she wouldn't have it if she was totally useless. Would she?

'We'll knock up a bit, first,' said Jonty, 'and then decide how we're going to play. We can always swap about if we're too badly matched.' I began to feel a bit anxious.

The noise of racquet on ball was suddenly right beside us. We'd reached a tarmac court surrounded by a mesh fence. It was nice and flat, but the lines were faded, especially around the service areas, and there were a few holes in the net. Christopher was picking up balls in the far corner with his back to us, but I watched as he straightened up and waved and came over. I saw another lanky lad who looked just like the boys in my class – hair so short you could hardly tell what colour it was; T-shirt and baggy shorts; grubby trainers. Nothing special.

'Christopher, hi!' said Jonty. 'This is Holly. Tamara's not here yet.'

Christopher loped over to greet us. 'So you're the famous Christopher!' I babbled, gushing nervously. Christopher looked at me, but he didn't reply. His jaw simply dropped. He glanced at Jonty questioningly.

'Heard you – playing – man, but never seen you in the flesh,' said Jonty. 'And I always seem to be telling Holly about you.' Christopher looked at the ground suddenly. He grunted something but didn't seem able to raise his gaze and look me in the eye. I wondered if the guy actually physically *couldn't* speak, and I hadn't been told, but Jonty punched him on the shoulder and said, 'Let's knock up. Whichever girl is more useless gets to play with you.' He whacked his racquet against a couple of balls lying on the ground and bounced them up to waist height. Clever, that. Took my mind off the insult. 'Come on, Hol! You play with me anyway until Tamara comes. We'll keep old Christopher here on the run.'

I realised early on that it was hardly worth my while joining in. Jonty and Christopher hit the ball low and hard to the baseline. From time to time they came up to the net and slammed the ball so fast I didn't have time to see it. Once or twice it arrived in my side of the court, but my nought to sixty acceleration is poor, and by the time I'd run for the ball it was too late. One time it hit me on the head and another on the backside. 'Perhaps I'd better sit out until Tamara comes,' I said, never thinking I'd actually look forward to her arriving on the scene. I didn't wait for a reply, but sat down near the mesh door of the court and took a swig at the bottle of Evian we'd brought with us. I watched the boys. Jonty was a good sportsman, and he played tennis as beautifully as he did everything else. But it was easy to see that Christopher had the makings of a champion. He might have looked like the boys at my school, but whereas they droop around not quite knowing what their legs are for, Christopher bounced and darted all over the court. He was always there, almost before Jonty had returned the ball, and his reactions were bullet-fast. Jonty started to flag, just a little, after five minutes of this, but Christopher was clearly only just beginning to warm up. I didn't know whether I wanted to be more useless than Tamara or not!

And here she was, along with Flavia and Beatrice, now both in full riding gear. The two older girls didn't stop. Her duty done by Tamara, Flavia led Beatrice off to the stables and the joys of Arnie and Sylvester. Tamara said 'Ciao' to the boys, who carried on playing, before peeling off her tracksuit trousers to reveal a tiny skirt, frilly knickers and the skinniest little pair of legs you've ever seen. Their rally over, Jonty and Christopher came to join us at the net post. Christopher actually managed to growl 'Hi Tamara.' Needless to say, Tamara didn't respond.

Jonty – I do love him for being so kind – said, 'You play with me then, Tamara, and we'll see how we go. Nice racquet,' he added, as she slid one of them out of the double case.

'Yah,' said Tamara, and trailed silently after him to the baseline.

I had as much trouble getting a word out of Christopher, though I'm sure in his case it was shyness rather than rudeness. He just wouldn't look me in the eye. I prattled away – 'Wow, hope I don't let you down by being atrocious. I don't really play, you know, just at school and with my dad, I've never played a real match before' – etc, etc. He just nodded and pointed to where I should stand. Aagh! Right by the net.

We knocked up a bit more. Tamara's stupid little knees pointed inwards when she ran and she never got to the ball once. I started to feel mildly superior as I returned Jonty's kindly angled gentle shots, but then the boys decided we should play a game. Christopher spun his racquet and Jonty called out 'Smooth' as it landed.

'Smooth it is,' said Christopher. He had no problem talking to Jonty, though he spoke quite softly.

'OK,' said Jonty. 'I'll serve first. OK, Tamara?'

'We'll stay this end,' said Christopher. He walked over to the right-hand corner, and gestured me to the net again with his racquet.

Jonty sent a sizzling service that squealed past my elbow. Christopher returned it to Tamara who simply stood and watched it, saying 'Eeuuu'.

Jonty swapped sides and I moved back to receive his serve. He sent me a gentle one, bless him, and I also hit it at Tamara, who missed it completely again, and said 'Eeuu.'

Jonty swapped sides again and served another sizzler to Christopher. Christopher made sure he returned it to Jonty this time and the two of them got quite a rally going while I crouched at the net feeling terrified and Tamara stood upright looking all around her. A volley came straight at me and I wopped it back instinctively. 'Well done!' yelled Jonty. He was racing all over the court while Tamara carried on standing there. Christopher and I won that game. We won Christopher's serve too. We even won mine – my service isn't very stylish but I can get it in.

And then it was Tamara's turn to serve. This was how she did it. First she removed a ball from the ridiculous clip she had round her waist. She held it up against the racquet. Then she brought both arms down in a circular motion, drew the racquet back dramatically, threw the ball a centimetre into the air and, piff, hit it into the net. A little scowl crossed her spoiled features as she frowned at her racquet and geared herself up to try again. But on her second serve she did exactly the same, except that she missed the ball altogether. It was hilarious, especially with Christopher bouncing and swaying, knees bent, in a very professional manner as he waited to receive it. We won that game too, to love (in other words, they didn't get a single point). In fact Christopher and I won the whole set to love. It was hardly due to me, but at least I hit the ball a few times – unlike Tamara. But was she abashed? Not a bit of it. At the end of the set she sat down with a bottle of water and pulled her second racquet from the case. As if it would make any difference! Jonty threw himself down beside me. 'Well played, my lovely!' he said, pulling my ponytail affectionately. Another resounding silence from our respective partners.

So we solemnly played a second set, the boys doing what they could, Tamara wallying about in her knock-kneed, mimsy fashion. I don't think she hit the ball once, not ever. Christopher and I won this set six-love, too. 'I'm whacked,' I said. 'Why don't you two boys have a game without us. We'll observe and learn, won't we Tamara?' I was trying to be friendly, honest I was, but she looked at me wordlessly, as usual, same vacant expression, mouth hanging slightly open. She sat down next to me and we were spectators as the boys played quite a reasonable game. Christopher won most of the points, but Jonty usually made him work for them.

I didn't know what to do with Tamara. I've just never met anyone like her before. However hard I tried, she blanked me. A phrase that amused my parents went through my head – 'Not quite our class, dear' – and I honestly think that's how she saw me. I'm used to posh people; after all, Dad teaches in a public school and I get to see the boys and their parents all the time, but here I was on a nice sunny day sitting by a tennis court next to a girl my own age and we had nothing to say to each other. I racked my brains, and suddenly I remembered my conversation with Dilly the night before: 'shopping – it's all they do,' was what she'd said. 'And barely a neurone between them.' Shopping. I took a punt. 'Harvey Nix is much better since they got that new bit,' I said casually. (I was winging it, but I've watched *Absolutely Fabulous*).

Bingo!

'Yah. Tons. Went there yesterday. Bought a top.'

'Great. What make was it?'

'Calvin Klein actually.'

'Ooh. What colour?'

'Difficult to say really.' (She said 'ralleh'.)

More silence, but you can't accuse me of not trying. I went back to watching the boys.

Midday, and it was too hot to do anything. We trooped back to the kitchen, pausing of course for Tamara to zip her racquets into their bag and gather up her classy track suit before heading into the cool of the rhododendrons. Jonty was very efficient in the kitchen, rustling up a big jug of squash with ice for us all and then digging out crisps and bread and cheese, a bag of salad, a tub of hummus and some tomatoes, with pots of yoghurt and peaches for afters. I was impressed. 'Does your Dad realise that you're a mean hand in the catering department, Jonty? Who needs Mrs B.?'

'I choose to keep those particular lights hidden under a bushel,' said Jonty. 'Anyway, it's Mrs B. that needs us. And hot stuff and puds are what she's a whizz at. Can't match her there.' There was no irony in his voice.

'We have au pairs for cooking,' said Tamara, 'but Mummy always tells them what to do.' No irony there, either. 'Last nanny left when Bea was fourteen.'

Didn't these people do *anything* for themselves? I looked over at Christopher but he was eyes down as usual. We ate our way through the meal. No one said much – most of the noise came from the ice cubes in the squash jug and the rustling of crisp packets.

Christopher was the first to get up. 'I'm going home, man,' he said to Jonty. 'Promised Mum I'd do the lawn today. She'll be on at me if I don't. I'll be back this evening with my brother, if that's OK.'

'Sure,' said Jonty. 'Wish we could all go for a swim as well, but I'm afraid the pool's still out of action. Ma's got the guy who does it working on something else at the moment.'

'See you,' said Christopher.

'Yeah, see you later,' Jonty and I said together.

Tamara was silent. But not for long. When Christopher had gone she drawled at Jonty, 'You could swim at Bury Hall.'

'Where's that?' I asked. 'Is it a sports centre or something?'

Oh naïve me. 'It's Tamara's house,' said Jonty. 'Thanks Tamara. Might take you up on that some time.' He stood up. 'Have to make do with a shower right now, though. There's one in the downstairs loo if you want, Tamara. See you both back here in quarter of an hour?'

'And then we'll see my sister and the horses, yah?' said Tamara.

I whizzed up to my *own* bathroom for a shower. What bliss! Afterwards I changed and sat down with my diary for five minutes.

Monday afternoon
Played tennis this morning with Jonty, the ghastly Tamara and the silent Christopher. He's OK (Christopher, that is). Not ugly or anything. And ace at tennis. But he doesn't say a word. Not to me at any rate. Which is a pity, because sometimes I think Jonty and Tamara are from a different planet from me – what with nannies and gardeners and horses and tennis courts and private swimming pools – whereas I get the feeling that Christopher leads a slightly more normal life. Still, at least Jonty's behaviour is normal. He's so patient with those awful girls, though. Sometimes I wish he was a bit nastier – I end up feeling a right bitch because I just want to hit them!

Ho hum. We're off to see the horses now. They've said I can have a ride if I want, but I suspect we're looking at classier horses than old Crisp at the riding stables! Or that trekking pony I loved so much on the school trip – Bonker? Conker? Question is, do I put on riding boots?

More tonight!

We met up in the kitchen. Tamara sat there turning through a copy of *Hello!* magazine. She'd obviously spurned the shower in the downstairs loo (I'd seen it earlier – it was a bathroom really, with the shower in a proper cubicle, heated towel rail, etc.), not that she'd exerted herself enough to work up anything approaching a sweat. Just looking at her in her OTT tennis gear made me feel irritated. I wanted Jonty to come and give me a hug right then, but he didn't. So I went and put my arm round his waist.

'OK, you two,' said Jonty, taking control. (*Not sure that I like being 'you two' with Tamara.*) 'Let's go and find the horses. Follow me.' Neither of them wore riding boots, so I just hoped we weren't actually expecting to *ride*.

'I know the way,' said Tamara unnecessarily – I think she was trying to get back at me somehow by rubbing in the fact that I was an outsider. 'Unless the stables have moved in the last year, that is.'

I wasn't having her queening it over me, and I certainly didn't want her sucking up to Jonty. So I grabbed him by the hand and wouldn't allow him to shake me off. 'You'll have to lead me,' I said. At least that way I wasn't the one trailing behind.

We cut across the fields to the side of the drive and then on to another lane that led off the road. The fields were full of molehills and nettles, and I got stung once or twice. I kept quiet though, because I realised that Tamara must be getting stung too, and muddying her white trainers – and she wasn't fussing. A sort of doggedness there. The lane led to the stables. There was dung in the road and horseflies. We walked down to the yard where Beatrice and Flavia were unsaddling Arnie and Sly. They were giggling and chatting with the stable lads. Flavia was tossing her jockey's name into the conversation at every possible opportunity. It never meant anything to me, but Beatrice and the lads were obviously impressed. So was Tamara. She overheard the conversation and said, 'So your boyfriend, yah? – the one we met? – he's *the* Gil Smith? Cool.'

'Never mind that he's pint-sized and ugly and doesn't have a chin,' said Jonty to me under his breath. It was good to have him back on my side again. The other three girls were yahing and snorting at each other, so Jont took me on a tour of the horses. There were eight of them. Arnie and Sky looked big to me, but Bluebottle (black) and Gorse (dun) were vast and Winslow (chestnut) and Shakespeare (dapple grey) were even vaster.

'They're huge,' I said.

'They're only hunters,' said Jonty. 'D'you fancy a ride? They're not neurotic, these fellows, but they go like the clappers once the chase is on.'

'Do you have anything – er – smaller?' I asked.

'Oh, but it's great being high up,' said Jonty, 'don't you think?'

'I wouldn't know.'

'But I thought you rode, Hol. You said you'd ridden quite a bit.'

'Depends how you see it. I had some riding lessons when I was little. And I've been trekking a few times . . .' I started to trail off. 'But I was quite good at it,' I added lamely. 'And I've brought my riding gear. Well, it used to be my cousin's . . .'

Jonty was looking at me. 'Ah,' he said. He thought for a while. 'Don't worry,' he added kindly. 'If you want to ride, you shall. There are quite a few younger kids who've just started to come on the hunt – I'm sure we can borrow one of their ponies. Ma can ring round tonight. We'll get you fixed up. A riding picnic's one of the things I've been looking forward to. There's this place I really want to show you, but you can only reach it on horseback – it's a bit too far to walk.'

Flavia, Beatrice and Tamara joined us. Tamara was patting the horses and being all soppy with them. 'How's my gorgeous Bluebottle?' sort of thing. I can't believe she can ride a horse that size, though she's a bit taller than Flavia.

Gorse bent his head down to Flavia and nuzzled her shoulder. 'Gorse, my baby,' said Flavia. 'Are you missing Dilly, then?'

'Does Dilly ride that great beast?' I asked, impressed.

'He's Dilly's horse,' said Flavia. 'She might not object if you rode him.'

'Holly was hoping for a smaller pony,' said Jonty quickly.

'Oh,' said Flavia. It came out as a bark.

'There's always Nibbles,' said Beatrice, with a sneaky grin.

'Nipples?' I asked, incredulous. (It's the way she talks, honest – like the Queen.)

'*Nib-bles!*' Tamara enunciated patiently, as if I was very young indeed. 'Used to be my pony, but I've outgrown him and no one rides him much these days, poor darling.'

'Sounds more my cup of tea,' I said.

Tamara was getting quite chatty now. 'You could come over to Bury tomorrow, Jonty,' she said. (I had to assume I was included in the invitation.) 'Have a ride and a swim.'

I could see Beatrice and Flavia looking at her, appalled. 'Are you inviting *those* two over to Bury?' Beatrice asked her rudely.

'Flavia could come too.' Tamara wasn't backing down. 'I don't see why I shouldn't ask people over. You always do.'

'Yes, but—'

'Cool,' said Jonty. 'We'll come, won't we Holly?'

Five

Tuesday morning, early

I have to sort my thoughts out. It's good to write them down.

There's this whole world that I don't understand. I have a dad who's a teacher, a mum who's a part-time nurse. I have a younger sister and a cat and a guinea pig. We live in a three-bedroomed house with a small garden. My friends live fairly close. We can hang around together, go window-shopping, go to the swimming pool, go horse-riding even – whatever – all for a price, but not that much. If we go swimming we can't go for a pizza; cinema, can't go clubbing; buy two tops, can't afford shoes. We share the chores (well, Mum does do most of the housework, but I try and do my bit – sometimes) and there's certainly no treasure like Mrs B.

And here I am with people who can't begin to understand my incredibly ordinary life. I said earlier that I think Christopher probably does, but he doesn't seem to want to speak to me, so how will I ever find out?

Actually that's not quite true. Jonty wanted to ride yesterday evening, and there isn't a horse for me. And then Christopher wanted to knock up with Jonty because his little brother was doing something else. So I ended up playing tennis with Christopher. Well, hardly playing exactly, but he told Jont it was good practice for him to place shots where I could get them, and it was certainly good practice for me. I was running around like a maniac, so it didn't matter that he barely spoke – I was too puffed to chat anyway. I think I was right before, and he's just shy with me. Can't think why.

Today we're all going over to Bury for a ride, followed by lunch and then a swim. It's all rather jolly hockey-sticks (not that Tamara and Beatrice are jolly anything) and organised, but hey, I am in another world. Jonty's still incredibly cute – though I wish he'd be a little less cute with T – it makes me think he's not picky enough. J and I had a nice smoochy time last night watching TV in a room on our own. Good job no one came in.

Went up to bed fairly early – Jonty will have got up early again to go and ride his racehorse at Lotbourne. (I hate to admit it, but Jonty is quite set in his ways. He won't not ride, just because I'm here. The horses and the life that goes with them are simply in his blood in a way that I wouldn't have thought possible. It's the bit I understand least about him, and I kind of wish he'd be a bit more flexible.) I'm not sure what we'll do between breakfast and going to Bury, but I'm not going down there until I hear Jonty come in. I don't want to be stuck with any of the others over the Sugar Puffs. Right, I can hear him coming in now, so down I go. It's 10.30 again – v. slothful but what the heck.

Flavia drove us to Bury Hall. It's a gorgeous house. Not as big as Clermont Chase, but with far more modern bits built on at the back, including this incredible pool – indoor, with huge glass sliding doors that you can open. Tamara was dressed for riding in jeans and a top, but Beatrice was in full sun gear and shades. She and Flavia went straight off to tan themselves on the patio outside the pool. Jonty and I followed Tamara, laden with tack, to the field where the ponies were. I spotted Nibbles miles away, a stout little bay pony with a pretty face, like a New Forest pony. The other two were considerably larger. 'They're not hard to catch,' said Tamara casually.

'Jonty!' I hissed. 'I can't catch a pony! Help me!' Tamara was already off after her pony, Skippy, who looked a bit lively to me, but good old Nibbles stood stock still, nibbling the grass.

Jonty walked up to him and slipped the halter over his neck, making it all look so easy, and walked him back to the yard. He put the saddle on and tightened the girth. He helped me fix the chin strap on my hard hat and gave me a kiss, making me feel a bit weak. 'OK then. You want to get on?' He stood by to help, but I knew he wanted to get going.

'Sure,' I said. It was a while since I'd done this – but I reckoned that it was probably something you didn't forget – like riding a bicycle. It isn't. I put my right foot in the stirrup, didn't I, and then realised that I'd end up facing the wrong way if I carried on. And then I couldn't untangle my foot. I was going to have to admit that I hadn't got a clue. I was sure I'd be all right once I was on his back. Tamara was already cantering around – show-off – and Nibbles looked like he wanted to join in. 'I'm sorry, Jont,' I said. 'I don't seem to be much good at anything, do I?'

'I can think of lots of things you're good at.' Jonty smirked as he helped me on to the pony's back. 'There. OK now?'

'I think so,' I said nervously. And Jonty was off again to saddle the big white – sorry, grey – pony.

Well, I stayed on. Some of those early lessons came back to me. Shoulders, hips, heels. Rise to the trot. Show who's boss. Well, the boss was definitely Nibbles. Mostly what Nibbles wanted to do was eat. The other two were up ahead looking dead professional. Annoyingly, Tamara looked a lot better on horseback than on the tennis court, but she still seemed strangely lethargic. I should have known that Jonty would look dashing on a horse. I remembered all over again why I fancied him. I almost wished I could be a damsel in distress.

Jonty twisted around in his saddle to check on me. I imagined how I must look, my feet almost touching the ground on this fat little pony – just like a Thelwell cartoon and not the slightest bit romantic. Jonty waved and then turned back to Tamara. Nibbles plodded along behind. But I was enjoying myself. We ambled through the woods, Nibbles and I. Every now and then he did a little trot to keep up with the others. I just clutched on to the reins with one hand and the saddle with the other until the trotting was over. We had to cross a stream at one point. I watched in horror as Jonty and Tamara jumped it, though luckily old Nibbles wasn't half as ambitious and simply picked his way through it, surefooted amongst the rocks and stones. It was beautiful, with dragonflies hovering over the water.

It was only a short ride (by their standards) because Tamara wanted to do some jumping. I'd had enough by the time we got back to the field, so I slipped off Nibbles, all on my own, and even managed to remove the saddle before letting him go and graze again. Jonty and Tamara were going round a little course of jumps. Tamara was efficient, but Jonty just seemed to fly. It's funny, isn't it, all these skills that you don't rate until you try them yourself? I could feel snooty about Tamara and Beatrice and Flavia because I felt they were so utterly deficient as human beings, but their ability to manage these great beasts certainly raised them a bit in my esteem. As for Jonty – he was a cool human being *and* an ace rider. I narrowed my eyes as I observed him with Tamara. I didn't want him being any nicer to her than was absolutely necessary.

We were all hot and thirsty. Tamara's mother was there when we got back. I'd expected someone thin and languid, if I'd expected anything at all, but she was short and bossy with thick glasses and wearing an extraordinary outfit – a velour sundress in jade green.

'Jonathan, dear! How nice to see you again after all this time. Goodness, you're a fine young man now!' She peered at me over her spectacles. 'Introduce me to Dilly's little friend. Holly, is it? Welcome to Bury Hall, dear.' I couldn't make her out at all. 'There's bread and salads on the patio table. Help yourselves and then come over to the barbecue.' Crikey. This was Organised City, Arizona.

Jonty loved it. 'Ace food, Mrs Hilton.'

'Call me Judy,' she simpered. 'I know how hungry you big boys get.' Clearly her skinny girls don't get hungry. She hovered over us while we filled our plates. Then I saw her game. 'That's right Jonathan, have as much as you want. Holly – these are the less calorific ones. I like my girls to eat sensibly for me, so I make sure there's always something they won't turn their noses up at. Tamara – I've done some vegan burgers for you, dear. Flavia and Bea, I think you'll find something you like over here.' Fuss, fuss, fuss.

The food was great and the puds were amazing (not that Tamara went anywhere near them). As usual, no one said much, except for Jonty and Mrs Hilton – Jonty congratulating and Mrs Hilton clucking. Flavia and Beatrice snorted a bit and Tamara whined once or twice. I just stuffed myself. When we'd finished, Jonty was effusive with his appreciation but the girls went back to the serious business of sunbathing. I stripped off to my yellow bikini and joined them. Barbados gave me a great tan and I was quite happy to show it off. Flavia is so fair-skinned you wouldn't know she'd been anywhere exotic and the Hiltons had spent most of the summer so far with their grandmother in Scotland, so they were gratifyingly white too. Which meant Tamara was white *and* skinny. In fact, Tamara in designer swimwear was a truly grisly sight. Beatrice and Flavia weren't much better. In the bikini stakes I felt self-confident again. Jonty came and sat shoulder to shoulder with me – he had a gorgeous Barbados tan too. It gave us a bond. I found myself giggling ostentatiously. I wanted Tamara to know that Jonty was *mine*. I wanted her mum to know that I wasn't 'Dilly's little friend' – I was the *girlfriend* of Jonathan (now a young man). What's more, I was brown and healthy-looking and not anorexic like her horrible daughters – even if I couldn't ride a horse. Believe me, I'm not usually catty, but this lot had that effect on me.

We had a swim once our lunch had gone down and then went out to sunbathe for a bit longer. Mrs Hilton brought home-made lemonade for us – 'far better for you than all those e-numbers, dears. I think the right food's *so* important, don't you?' Flavia and Bea disappeared off, for a cigarette I suspect. Jonty and I had another swim – just the two of us, which was great, and then it was time to go home to Clermont Chase. I was glad to say goodbye to the Hiltons. Nice house. Shame about the owners.

Jont and I separated for showers before dinner. I like this little gap of time to myself in the evening. I'd never normally shower at this time, but after all our various exertions it seemed a good idea. I might even try and keep it up when I get home. Good diary-writing time, too.

Tuesday afternoon

Went over to Bury, Tamara's house, for a ride and lunch and a swim today. I managed to ride T's old pony, Nibbles, without falling off, so I'm quite pleased with myself. Mrs H is a terrible fusspot but she gave us a good lunch and J and I were able to shake T off for a bit in the pool. She was with us all the rest of the time. She's really, really ghastly and whiny and I don't know what J sees in her. What am I saying? I don't think he does see anything in her, but she obviously fancies the pants off him and he doesn't seem to mind. I couldn't stand it if someone that repellent fancied me – I'd want to tell him to bog off. But J just isn't like that. I do sometimes wonder about him being so laid back and nice to everyone. I mean, it's what I like about him – but if I'm honest, it's what I don't like about him, too. It was different in Barbados. I thought he was nice to me because I was special. Now I'm not sure. Maybe that was just his manner, and I misinterpreted it. Still, there are worse faults than being nice, I suppose!

I get another game of tennis with Christopher after supper tonight. It's quite a neat arrangement. I wish Jonty was as jealous of C as I am of T, but I couldn't do that to him, and anyway I don't fancy C and he barely says a word to me and still won't look me in the eye. Why not?

Supper was microwaved stuff that didn't taste of anything, with ice cream for afters. Gina wasn't around, so the other three did the microwaving. Brian smacked his lips as usual and said it was delicious and then Jont went off to ride, Flavia went to phone Gil, her jockey, and I went off to meet Christopher for a tennis practice.

Christopher was already there, surrounded by millions of tennis balls, serving them as hard as he could. 'That looks dangerous!' I called, ducking exaggeratedly.

'Huh,' he said, and gave the tiniest of smiles. Then he pointed me to the baseline and started potting some soft shots over for me to return. We did this for an hour. Sometimes he indicated with gestures that I should practise volleying at the net, or returning lobs from the baseline, but I couldn't get a word out of him. I gave up trying. I watched him instead. I learned a lot. I saw how quickly he took his racquet back, how he bent his knees, bounced about, never for one moment took his eye off the ball. And when I started concentrating as hard as he did it really started to show. When we came off he wiped his forehead on his sleeve and said (without looking at me), 'You're improving.' Then his mouth clamped shut.

'Thanks,' I said, thinking he was going to go off home. But he came with me.

'Got to fetch some flowers for my mum,' he said. (Hey, long sentence.)

I saw my opening. 'She does all the fantastic flower arrangements, doesn't she?' I said. 'She's a real artist.'

'Yes,' said Christopher.

He saw me looking at him questioningly. 'Yes, I mean she is a serious artist. That's what she does. Gina pays her for the flower arranging. It all helps.'

What do you say to that, from someone who has barely uttered a word until now? 'What sort of thing does she do?' I tried.

'She's a – feminist artist,' he said, his eyelids lowered. 'You'd have to see for yourself.'

'I'd love to,' I said, wondering what on earth he meant.

We walked on in our more customary silence. There was Jonty. 'Christopher, hi! You coming in for a drink? I know Ma's got some flowers for you to take home.'

We all went down the passage to the kitchen. Flavia,

Gina and Brian were sitting over gin and tonics. They were talking quite heatedly. Jonty fetched us Cokes and we joined them.

'I blame their mother,' said Flavia. 'She's so hung up about "the right" food. No wonder Tamara has eating problems.'

'She's a perfectly ghastly woman, I agree,' said Gina, going over to the sink that was filled with flowers and starting to roll huge bunches of them in newspaper.

'She's not ghastly,' said Jonty stoutly. 'She said I'd grown into a fine young man.'

'Well, she would,' said Flavia. 'She's so desperate to get her girls married off to fine young men that she's getting to work on you already.'

'And she's a good cook,' said Jonty.

'Precisely,' said Flavia. 'That's the problem.'

'I know Tamara's unhappy at school,' said Jonty. So that's what they'd been talking about. 'She gets bullied.'

Hardly surprising. I thought uncharitably, and then wished I hadn't.

'It's a jolly good school, by all accounts,' Brian said, looking up from the paper.

'Bea loved it,' said Flavia.

And then, without thinking, I said something really stupid. 'I think I'd be unhappy if I had to go to boarding-school.'

'Oh no, no, no,' said Brian, dismissing the concept out of hand. 'Good for the character. Never harmed anyone. Good practice for the real world.'

I wondered how I could change the subject – I'd temporarily forgotten I was in a room full of people who went or had been to boarding-school (apart from Christopher) and I didn't want to get in any deeper. But Brian had started and he was determined to carry on. 'Of course, it has to be one of the better ones. Some of them are worse than useless.'

'*I* sometimes wish I was at day school,' said Jonty. 'Like Christopher. Then I could ride every day.'

'But there aren't any decent ones locally,' Brian blundered on, ignoring the fact that Christopher must go to one that wasn't decent if that was the case.

'My dad teaches at a private day school,' I said helpfully.

'Oh, well, fine if you live in London,' said Brian. 'But not out here.'

'I suppose a good education is important,' said Jonty, trying not to side with anyone.

'Of course it is,' said Brian. 'Absolutely crucial.'

'It is if you want to go to a good university,' said Gina.

My mind was racing. I'd heard this argument so often, though from a different point of view. Dad loves the school he teaches at, but he has no qualms about sending his children to the local state schools. He says we're clever anyway, and it's better to be with one's peers of all sorts; there's more to learning than just academic subjects. And I do want to go to a good university. Dad went to Oxford from a state school. I wanted to say so many things. I didn't want to put my foot in it again but I couldn't let them get away with this sort of talk. 'I go to a comprehensive,' I said bravely. Silence.

'Well, I don't expect your parents mind too much about what university you go to,' said Brian, trying to be kind.

I wasn't having it. 'They jolly well do,' I fumed. 'I want to go to Sussex or Edinburgh.'

'Exactly,' said Brian.

I could feel myself getting worked up. 'Oxford and

Cambridge aren't the only good universities you know. And surely it isn't necessary to tear eight-year-olds away from their mothers just to perpetuate the system,' I said, echoing my father. 'Little kids should be at home. Tamara should be at home if that's where she wants to be.' I couldn't believe I was sticking up for her.

'Goodness me,' said Gina. 'Where *would* we all be if we simply let our children do what they wanted?' To be fair, she wasn't trying to put me down, she was trying to end a conversation that she could see was getting out of hand. 'Here are the flowers, Christopher. You'd better get them to Jill before they start to wilt on us. Shall I get some carriers for you? Now, Jonty, Holly, wasn't there something you wanted to watch on television?'

As Jonty hurried me off for another kissing session on the sofa (Gina isn't stupid) I heard Flavia saying to her father, 'What exactly do they *do* at a comprehensive?' I felt slighted and hurt, and I dare say Christopher did too, even though I knew they didn't mean to be insulting to either of us personally. Mum always says its best not to get caught up in debates about education. Everyone always likes to think they're doing the best thing for their children.

Jonty isn't stupid, either. 'Sorry about that, Holly. Pa and Flavia live in the dark ages. Ma doesn't. Part of the reason she didn't want that conversation to carry on was because she took me away from my prep school. I loathed it. Pa didn't forgive her until I was ensconced where I am now. He thought she was turning me into a wimp.'

'You're not a wimp, Jont. You're . . . just right.'

'I know,' he said smugly and pushed me back on the sofa. He sat up again. 'Bit worried about Tamara though. She does look anorexic.'

'I'll say,' I said too quickly.

'Oy, Holly, don't be mean!'

'Sorry,' I said, but again I couldn't let it go. I should have done – he'd as good as told me he felt sorry for her. 'You don't *like* her do you?'

'What do you mean, *like*? She's OK.'

'She's not OK. She's wimpy and whingey and spoilt.'

'Hey, Holly! Miaow! She's not that bad!'

'She is,' I said. 'And she fancies you,' I added. There, I'd really done it now.

'Naturally,' said Jonty. 'No one is impervious to my charms!' He pushed me back against the sofa again, but somehow the moment had passed, and all of a sudden the football on the TV seemed to interest him more than I did.

I wrote my diary before I went to sleep.

Tuesday night
I'm not a happy bunny. I think I've blown it. They were all sneering about comprehensives and I made an idiot of myself. Jonty obviously likes Tamara and I'm stuck here for days yet. I feel so miserable. I love Jonty, he's so fantastic, but I can't seem to fit in. They make me feel so inferior – and bitchy too. All of them. Christopher actually spoke to me tonight. Apparently his mum is a 'feminist' artist. At least he's not a spoilt rich person. I'd like to go to his house and see his mum's work. We're off on some outing tomorrow. Can't remember where.

Six

The outing was to Stratford-upon-Avon. Jonty woke me with a cup of tea. He hadn't noticed that I don't drink tea, but never mind. He tried snuggling in with me, but since he was still in riding gear it wasn't very comfortable. Flavia also decided to station herself outside the door and shout to Gina so that we were aware of her. 'Mother? You want to leave soon don't you? What's the weather going to be like? Shall I hurry Jonty up?' She moved even closer to my door and yelled, 'Jonty! Come and have breakfast! Now!' Cow.

Jonty shot out and I got up in record time. Shame. I've enjoyed my leisurely mornings up until now. I arrived at breakfast feeling as if I'd already done something wrong. Not a good start. But Gina was all smiles today. 'Right. Cooked breakfast this morning. What would you like Holly? Jill's given me some eggs from her hens, so I'd recommend a boiled egg. Or would you prefer scrambled?'

I thought about Gina's cooking. 'I'd love a boiled egg.'

'Me too,' said Jonty.

'Flavia?'

'Yah.'

Gina had poured the orange juice into a jug. There was toast cooling off in a toast rack. She put a pan of water on to boil and sat down with us. 'Now today the Estate Office can go hang because today is polo day and I also want to be a good hostess and show Holly some of the sights. So – ' she stood up to check the pan of water and carried on speaking as she lowered the eggs in –

'we're going to Stratford. Sightseeing first, before all the grockels arrive. That's for you two while I get my hair cut. Picnic lunch by the river at Charlcote – ' she patted a picnic hamper. 'Afternoon watching polo, supper in the theatre and then *As You Like It*?'

'Wow!' I said. 'It sounds wonderful.' It did. I'd never been to Stratford-upon-Avon. Maybe it wasn't so bad staying here after all. And a day without Tamara! Gina doled out the boiled eggs. 'I want to be off before ten,' she said. 'Be out by the car – we'll take the Range Rover.' She went out of the kitchen, trailed by three hopeful dogs. Flavia made her egg into a sandwich and wandered off with it, leaving Jonty and me alone with our nursery breakfast of soft-boiled eggs and toasty fingers. I wanted to say something about the joy of a whole day without Tamara for a change, but I thought better of it. I was going to be my usual friendly self today, not the catty person that Tamara made of me. I half-wondered too if they were compensating for putting me down last night, but somehow I doubted it. I don't honestly think they're conscious that they're doing it.

'Do you think I should wear something different, Jonty? I'd no idea we were going to the theatre as well.' I was wearing shorts and a top.

'Ma won't mind. Dad likes my sisters to dress up, but he's not coming. Flavia will probably get tarted up for the polo, though. Yeah, go on, wear one of your skirt things. I'm just wearing *clean* shorts, a *clean* T-shirt and my less scruffy trainers.' We went our separate ways to change. Someone came to the door while we were going upstairs and Flavia answered it, but I never found out who it was.

Flavia didn't come with us – she was meeting up with

Gil and joining us for the polo – so Jonty and I sat up in the front of the Range Rover with Gina. She drove fast but I felt safe with her – it was fun being so high up. We arrived in Stratford ahead of the rush of coaches and Gina went to have her hair done while Jonty took me off round the sights. It's a pretty town but I couldn't believe how touristy it was. Everything was half-timbered. Everyone was cashing in. We went to Shakespeare's birthplace and I tried to imagine it as it must have been but I couldn't make the leap. Does everyone have this problem with historic houses? I could imagine him peeping over the window-ledge at the house over the road, and maybe crawling up the stairs, but nothing else made me feel he'd really lived there. (Anyway, was Shakespeare ever a *baby*?) Jonty'd been loads of times before, so he was past that stage. 'Cool shop here,' he said. 'Have you got to buy presents for anyone?'

'Not really, I brought them all things from Barbados. I'll get some postcards to send to my friends though. Shall we do one together for Maddy?'

'Aah. Gorgeous Maddy.'

'Jonty!'

'Well, she was pretty, wasn't she?'

'Jonty! Ahem! Are we forgetting something here?'

'Well, you're pretty too, but you know what I mean.'

'And how would you feel if I went all starry-eyed about Red?' (Red was Maddy's boyfriend in Barbados, and yes, he was amazing-looking.)

'Well, we can't all look like film stars.'

'My point precisely.'

'Only joking, Hol. Lighten up?' He tilted my chin up so that I looked him in the eye. 'We're going to enjoy today, OK?'

'OK. I just get a complex if you start fancying other girls. Especially blondes.'

'Well, I won't today.' This wasn't quite the answer I required. 'It's just us. No skinny Tamara, no bossy older sisters and no lovesick Christophers.'

'Lovesick? What do you mean?'

'D'you mean you hadn't noticed?'

'Noticed what?'

'That he blushes and goes completely tongue-tied when he's around you?'

'I just thought he was . . . I just thought he was a silent sort of guy.'

'Christopher? Oh no, Ms Davies, that is the effect you are having on him.'

'I don't know what to say. Has he said anything to you?'

'What do you think? Course he hasn't. But I can tell he's jealous as hell. We blokes know these things. Isn't it great? Usually I'm the one who's envious of him.'

'So where does this leave me?' We were standing in the little garden just before the shop. Jonty threw his arms around me and sweetly touched his lips against my forehead and my nose before kissing me. People were looking at us.

'As my very own gorgeous Holly who has a beautiful face, huge eyes, lovely hair and a fabulous body.'

'Jonty!'

'I don't care! Stop worrying about other people!'

Oh my god – I just knew he was about to do something embarrassing. He was. He went down on one knee and started spouting Shakespeare: 'Shall I compare thee to a summer's day? Thou art more lovely and more temperate, et cetera . . . There, do you believe me now?'

A couple of American tourists in Bermuda shorts and

baseball caps started to clap. I was blushing frantically. Jonty adored playing to the gallery. At least he hadn't swept me up in a tango like he did with Maddy in Barbados.

'So just remember, OK? Now, let's go and buy a postcard for the stupendously ugly Maddy. Then we can go and have a drink in that coffee shop and wait for my mother.'

I was intrigued by the idea of Christopher liking me, but I didn't understand it, and I certainly couldn't talk to Jonty about it. And since any bloke would fancy Maddy, and he did call Tamara skinny, I tried to banish all jealous thoughts for the day.

We were having milkshakes and blueberry muffins when Gina arrived and decided to have exactly the same herself. She was a weird lady, and certainly a peculiar sort of mother, but there was something a bit wild and bohemian beneath her steely exterior and I felt that I could grow to like her. Strange, because I'm not used to seeing grown-ups as people! When she had finished she looked at her watch. 'Goodness! Is that the time? Would you two mind awfully if we gave Charlcote a miss and had our picnic at the polo? I promise we'll have our supper by the river. I'll ring now and reserve one of the riverside tables.' She pulled a phone out of her bag, and steamrollered the restaurant into reserving a special table. I couldn't imagine my mum doing that!

Then we emerged into the midday heat and walked to the Range Rover which was like an oven until the air-conditioning came on. Gina drove us to the horses. I've never been to anything horsy before. We parked in rows in a field, where loads of people had already set up their picnics, with champagne and salmon and everything, all balanced on little picnic tables. Most of them were quite smartly dressed and looked incredibly posh (I think I even recognised a minor royal – 'Almost certainly,' said Jonty – exciting or what?), so I was glad I'd made a bit of an effort with my clothes. The atmosphere was very friendly though. Gina buys a good picnic. She spread out one of those waterproofed tartan rugs and sat us down with all sorts of quiches and pies, French bread, French cheese, grapes, peaches. There was even chilled white wine which she pressed on us (not least because the only other drink she'd brought was tea in a Thermos). Then we went our separate ways, Gina to find Flavia, Gil and a polo pony that used to belong to them. Jonty and I pushed our way through the crowds to find a good place to watch. The wine had gone to our heads a bit, so we clung to each other and were glad when we found somewhere to settle. We sat back to back on the grass and dozed gently until the match began. It was blissful.

We were brought to our senses by the sound of a bell. And the commentator clearing his throat over the PA system. There was going to be a 'practice match' followed by the main one. Jonty explained that there were only four players on each side. There were yellow posts at either end and the teams hit a white ball around with the side of a long wooden-ended cane stick. I couldn't quite work out what was going on, but it was fun to see how the ponies bunched up until one managed to ride free. I decided to root for the yellow team and joined in the ra-ra-ra-ing and cries of 'Good shot!' from time to time. The bell rang every time someone scored a goal and they changed ends, so it was hard to keep up. They played four 'chukkas' – seven-

and-a-half minute 'quarters'. When the yellow team won 4–3, I was jumping up and down with the rest of them!

Then a whistle went and the commentator asked the crowd to come and 'tread in'. 'Follow me,' said Jont, and everyone went on to the pitch to tread the divots back in! 'You ain't seen nothin' yet,' said Jonty. 'They were just juniors. The next lot will blow your socks off.' Actually, the players alone blew my socks off. They were dead sexy, especially a couple of Argentinians, what you could see of them under the grilles of their helmets.

Jonty suddenly recognised one of the ponies. 'That's Pink Gin!' he said. 'Great – this will be a really cool match. Pink Gin was once one of our racehorses. Watch out for him, he could turn on a pound coin!' He was right, the second match was far more exciting. The horses thundered backwards and forwards, the mounted umpires chasing after them with their whistles. I just prayed that no one would fall off near us! Pink Gin's side won and Jonty, Gina, Flavia and Gil went mad when the players went up to fetch their prize champagne. The five of us trooped back to the Range Rover – for a few moments I felt quite elated and part of it. Then Gina drove us back into Stratford for our evening at the theatre. It was a lovely pink sort of evening – I was beginning to feel like someone in a film.

As soon as Gina swept into the theatre restaurant it was obvious that she was known. No one could have mistaken her for another American tourists. We don't eat out much at home beyond the odd pizza or Indian – and even that seems expensive when I sneak a look at the bill. Dad gets thrilled when the staff at our local Indian recognise him. Now the waiter led us to a table which was right by the river. Swans bobbed about on the water, hoping for crusts. We waved regally at passing cruisers and some of the other boats that slipped past, quietly shattering the reflections in the river. Gina said we could choose what we liked – have all three courses if we wanted (with Mum and Dad it's always starter *or* pudding) and any sort of drink, though not alcohol if we wanted to stay awake for the play.

She needn't have worried about me staying awake for the play. I was spellbound from the moment Orlando walked on to the stage. He was *gorgeous*! Really tall with dark curls and dark melting eyes. We had such brilliant seats (front row of the dress circle) that I could drool over him at close quarters. As if the polo players hadn't provided enough excitement for one day I fell completely in love. (At a distance, naturally. Sort of getting my own back for Tamara I suppose.) Forgetting about Jonty sitting beside me, I even felt jealous of Rosalind! Of course, they were all Sirs and Ladies, high-born gentlefolk with servants and big houses. How strange that Gina and Jonty should be living relics of all that. Still, Shakespeare had to work for a living. My thoughts were short, ragged things – my head was really taken up with the play. In the story Rosalind (a blonde, please note) sees Orlando wrestling and falls passionately in love with him (I'm not surprised), and he with her (damn). Orlando has been banished to the Forest where Rosalind and her cousin Celia (dark-haired) have also fled (well fancy that), dressed as a shepherd and a shepherdess. So then there's lots of cross-dressing fun in the woods until the end when Rosalind finally comes out as a girl and she and Orlando get hitched, along with Celia who has strangely fallen for Orlando's horrible brother. It was fabulous, and I loved every minute of it. *I* wanted to wander through the woods in a beautiful long dress and find my name carved on the trees. In fact I wanted to *be* Rosalind, *now*. Or the actress that played her every night.

Jonty had enjoyed the play too. As the actors took a final curtain call he gave a happy sigh and squeezed my hand. 'Enjoy it?'

'I'll say.' I leant over to Gina. 'Thank you so much Gina. It was wonderful.'

'It was a pleasure,' said Gina graciously. 'The bard rarely lets one down. I must say, I thought Orlando was frightfully handsome, didn't you?'

'He was gorgeous,' I said.

'Reminded me a bit of Christopher,' she said.

'Mother!' Jonty said. 'He looked nothing like Christopher.'

'He's had that awful prison haircut for so long that you forget he has curls,' said Gina. 'You both had curls when you were little and then yours turned to waves but Christopher's got curlier and he had them shaved off. Mothers adore curls.'

'Moth*er*!' said Jonty, getting to his feet, 'you're embarrassing me! How can I maintain my sophisticated macho image in front of Holly if you insist on talking about my lovely curly hair?'

'I was talking about Christopher's really,' said Gina.

I leant my head on Jonty's shoulder on the way back, imagining that he was Orlando, I'm afraid. I was sleepy as we drove home through the lanes, but Gina had given us a good day and I felt at ease with the Hayters again.

When we got back, Flavia and Gil were sitting up with Brian in the kitchen talking about the polo. Unlike me, Gina and Jonty knew what they were talking about and wanted to join in, but I wanted to go to bed. Jonty slipped out to kiss me goodnight. 'Fair Rosalind,' he teased. 'I know you wish I was that girly Orlando, but I'm glad you're you.' We kissed. 'Night, gorgeous,' he said, and then went back into the kitchen to join in the polo talk.

I made my way upstairs to the back of the house. I knew the way so well now. I opened the door to my room. It must have been Mrs B.'s day to do the bedrooms because it was all tidy, with my clothes in neat piles and the bed temptingly folded back. And the flowers were different. On the bed was a little pile of post and a parcel. The ballgown! Good old Daisy.

I'm one of these people who likes to save their treats, so I washed and changed into my nightie before starting on the mail. There was also a letter from my parents, carefully addressed to Ms Holly Davies, c/o Jonathan Clermont-Hayter, etc, and what looked like a letter from Dilly. Bumper post!

31 North Hill Road
London N.

Dear Holl-doll,
Thought you might like a letter, though I'm sure you're not the slightest bit homesick. I suppose this is all good practice for the French Exchange next year. I hope you're having a lovely time – the countryside must be so green and cool in this weather. Do they have a swimming pool? (shouldn't be surprised!). I'm dying to hear all about it. Do be polite and thank for things, won't you? If there's any possibility of going to Stratford, jump at the chance. I've heard there's a

terrific RSC performance of *As You Like It* on at the moment. If someone could get you there we'd be happy to pay for you and Jonty to see it (groundlings only, I'm afraid). I know you'd love it. See what you can do. Daisy has said she'll get the ballgown to you. If I've got the address right it will reach you at the same time as this.

Lots of love, darling. See you on Sunday,

M

How's life with the nobs then? Make sure they treat my little Holl-doll with the respect she deserves. You might not be an heiress but you have beauty and brains, a rare combination that Jonty obviously has the good taste to appreciate. Look forward to having you home again, sweetheart. Abby misses you and so do we.

Dx

Dear Holly,

Daddy has drunk a whole half bottle of wine so I think he feels a bit soppy. I hope you are having a nice time. I can't think what to say.

Lots of love from your adoring sister,

Abby

Aah. That letter did make me feel a bit homesick actually. Good old Mum. I felt almost disloyal for going to that very play and sitting in the most expensive seats when paying for them and for dinner must have meant so little to Gina. I put the letter firmly back in its envelope. I wouldn't want my hosts reading Dad's little contribution.

Second letter. From Dilly.

Hi Hol! Thought you might need a letter from me to get you through the week with my frightful family. I know you don't think Jonty's frightful, but you know how I feel about my little brother and perhaps you'll be of the same opinion by now. (Don't mean it really. He's quite cute, as little brothers go. Better than he used to be anyway.)

TIPS FOR VISITORS

Big sister: Keep out of her way. I can't stand her most of the time – she thinks she's so superior just because she's the oldest. I'm afraid you can't trust her to be nice.

Little brother: Typical male, arrogant and a pain. Only interested in sport. Charms the pants off old ladies. But you like him anyway, so I'll shut up.

Father: Fine and good natured as long as you don't engage him in conversation about a) politics b) education c) the EU d) the welfare state and e) blood sports.

Mother: Some of my friends don't understand Ma because she's not very mumsy and has some weird ideas. We get on fine because she mostly leaves me to my own devices. She'll like you, I know, because you've got a mind of your own.

Granny: You might or might not meet her – she was still away when I left and I'm not sure when she gets home. Granny doesn't understand the word 'can't.' She does what she wants and expects everyone else to do the same. She's quite cool as grannies go.

You can tell I'm bored. The others on this course aren't very interesting and the one guy I liked has gone off with a blonde bimbo. Don't you hate them?

Have you met Christopher yet? And his younger brother Toby? And his mum, Jill? I love Christopher to bits, always have done. He's been a bit like a brother to me so I don't fancy him. You might though – if you weren't going out with Jonty that is. He's deep, is Chris, so promise me you won't mess with him. And an ace tennis player too. I'd marry him if he was rich, but he's not, so he's safe from me!

Toby must be about twelve by now – looks identical to the way Chris looked before he shaved his hair off. He's a bit of a pain.

Jill: Wacko lady. Single mum, poor as a church mouse but brilliant artist. Granny buys her paintings but Mum's too embarrassed to have them on the wall. Have a look at them and you'll see why! (Does the name Georgia O'Keefe mean anything to you? Chris explained it all to me once.)

Who else? You said you'd been forced into the company of Tamara Hilton, Flavia's friend Beatrice's younger sister. Aagh. Poor you. I've never had to take any notice of her because she's Jonty's age (i.e. yours) not mine, but I can't stand either of them chiefly because they're so thick (huh – and thin!). Their house is quite nice and they've got a better pool than ours, especially since ours is out of action. Anyway, advice: avoid at all costs. It's supper time. Must go. Honestly, this is almost as bad as school except that there are boys, if you can call them that.
Love, Dilly.

My eyes were rolling up into my head I was so tired. The parcel could wait until morning – I couldn't be bothered to get out of bed and try a dress on anyway. I turned out the light and fell asleep.

Seven

It was Thursday already! I woke up knowing I had a treat in store, though when I checked my watch and realised it was 10.30 *again* I leapt out of bed like a scalded cat. I catapulted into the bathroom, had a shower, and then remembered my 'treat'. The ballgown! I shot back into the bedroom in my towel and tore open the parcel. Wow! Cousin Daisy could afford Monsoon! It was a full-works ballgown in fuchsia pink silk. The towel dropped off and I stepped into the dress. I paraded around feeling like a princess, my long dark hair tumbling down my naked back. I did a twirl in front of the mirror. I felt fabulous. I felt like Rosalind! I could see my name inscribed on all the trees of the forest already. Jonty would go ape!

The 'do' was tonight – wasn't it? No one had mentioned it, though I had seen the invitations, three of them, to Gina and Brian, Flavia and partner and Jonathan and partner, all gilt and deckled edges, tucked into the mirror. 'Black tie.' That meant evening dress, didn't it? The ball was in aid of some junior polo team. I shimmied out of the ballgown, enjoying the swish of the silk as it curtseyed to the ground. Shorts felt very mundane after that and it seemed almost criminal to scrape my hair back into a ponytail – I'd throw all the conditioners and stuff at it when I washed it for tonight. Exciting!

I was relieved to hear voices in the kitchen as I approached. Don't know why I worry so much. No one actually *cares* when I come down for breakfast – unlike at home where I can hear Mum and Dad saying, 'Isn't it time Holly was up? She's wasting the day!' most weekends! I pushed open the kitchen door. Jonty, Flavia and Gil were in there with Brian, still discussing the polo as if they'd never been to bed. Jonty came over to greet me. He was looking good this morning in a whiter than white T-shirt and pale Gap shorts and sun tan. The sunlight coming in through the kitchen windows caught the hairs on his arms and legs. He's not *hairy* hairy, just right. I couldn't wait to see him all dressed up tonight. Maddy said he'd looked pretty cool at the dance in Barbados. Envy, envy. Still, I was going to look darned cool too in my fuchsia silk. 'Morning, gorgeous! Rescue me from yet another blow-by-blow account of yesterday's match!'

'That's not fair,' said Brian mildly. 'I had to miss it.'

'Anyway,' said Flavia, 'it's interesting, isn't it Gil?'

'Problems Flavia?' said Gil, who'd actually taken the opportunity to glance at the paper.

'Yah,' said Flavia. 'My baby brother's accusing us of being boring.'

'Ahuh!' Gil did a funny sort of laugh.

'Eat!' Jonty pushed a plate in front of me. 'Jill dropped round some croissants she picked up from the bakery in the early hours of this morning. She's getting Granny's cottage ready for her.'

'Granny back today then?' asked Flavia.

'Yup,' said Jont. 'She's been terrorising Tuscany for far too long.'

'My friend Zoe went to Tuscany this year,' I said. 'She's pretty terrifying. Does your granny like a good argument?'

'*Oh* yes,' said Jonty. 'Nothing better.'

'Perhaps they met up,' I said.

'I doubt it, dear,' said Brian, diplomatic as always.

'Let's talk about something else,' said Jonty quickly.

'OK,' I said. 'Guess what was in my parcel?' I grabbed his arm. 'I have got *the* most fabulous dress for tonight.'

It worked. 'Must fly,' said Brian, unruffled, and left, just as Gina came in.

'Tonight?' said Jonty.

'Isn't it the dance thingy tonight?' I said.

'Yeah, it is,' said Flavia, interested, 'but Holly's not invited, is she, Jonathan?'

'I thought Jonty was invited,' I said. 'With partner.'

'He is, dear,' said Gina smoothly.

I looked from Gina to Flavia to Jonty. There was a deafening silence.

'So—'

Jonty couldn't look me in the eye. 'I have to go with Tamara,' he said.

'You *what*?'

Stupid old Flavia said, 'Well, I was the one who organised the tickets, so when Beatrice said her miserable little sister wouldn't shut up until someone got her a ticket I had to say she could go with my brother, didn't I? Can't imagine why she should want to. Jonty never told me he was going with Holly. And anyway, Judy Hilton's paid me for the tickets already.' Her voice was rising into a steady whine.

'Problems, Flave?' Gil looked up from his paper.

'No,' Gina cut in. 'Never mind, Holly. There'll always be another one. Judy Hilton seemed set on this for Tamara, I'm afraid – something to do with a dress the child has spent vast sums of money on. But you can spend the evening with Granny instead. You'll like that.'

My jaw dropped. I knew I was about to cry. What

about *my* beautiful dress? Daisy had gone to all that trouble to find it and post it.

Jonty tugged at my arm. 'Come on. It's not important. It's only a naff old dance for the polo club. Bring your croissant. Come outside with me. It's a brilliant morning out there.'

Once outside, Jonty marched me away from the house as quickly as possible. I thought he was going to grovel and apologise, but he really didn't think there was anything at issue here. He simply said, 'Sorry about all that. At least we've managed to spend most of the time together. One evening apart won't kill us.'

'But Jonty!' I wasn't having all this matter of factness. 'Jonty – why won't you let me tell you how I feel?'

'Because it won't make any difference?'

'Why won't it make a difference?'

'Because, between them, my family have made the decisions already, and there's no way they'll budge. If Flavia's done her friend Beatrice a favour by getting a ticket to keep her sister quiet, she won't go back on it.'

'But what about me? I was really looking forward to it. I've had a dress sent to me specially. I wanted to go with you, because you're my boyfriend.'

'Believe me, you're not missing anything. I go to loads of these things, with Dilly usually. Everyone dressed up like idiots. Loads of giggling girls. Crap band. Vile wine.'

'You go with Dilly?'

'Well, there's this partner thing. Dilly doesn't have much time for me on a regular basis, but I can dance and I look older than fourteen. Once we're in, she abandons me and goes off to pull on her own – someone else who's been dragged along by a sister.'

'And what about you?'

'I block my ears against the crap band and get tiddly on the vile wine. I can do it without throwing up now.'

He really didn't see it. 'Well, it would have been a real treat for me. I've never done anything like that before. I've never been to any sort of dance apart from the Christmas disco at school. And that's in the afternoon in a fully-lit classroom. And now you won't see me in the dress. I look OK in it.'

'Bet you do. Can I have a private showing?'

'That's not the same thing, and you know it.'

'You get to go to Granny's, and that's far better.'

'You are joking?'

'No. Granny's a gas. You'll see.'

'Hhhhmph.'

'Come on, let me take you on a tour of the Clermont follies. Some of them are *nice* and secluded, and we won't be disturbed.'

Well, despite my disappointment, he *was* looking sexy. I wanted to make sure it was me he was interested in and not Tamara. Folly number three was actually an old dovecote and it was cool after the heat outside. It was only about twelve feet across. We stood in the middle of it, rays of light coming in through the holes for the doves in a conical roof. Jonty put his hands on the bare bit between my shorts and my top. He's got big hands and I've got a little waist. They almost went right round. He pulled me to him for a kiss. We're good at kissing now – we can sort out our teeth and tongues without getting embarrassed or giggling. We can do it for hours. My legs started to feel all weak. Jonty's must have been as well. 'Let's lie down,' he said. The ground was dry. 'I'll take off my T-shirt – give us something to lie on.'

Somehow Jonty with a bare chest and shorts was even

sexier than Jonty in swimming things (probably because he'd taken his T-shirt *off*). I laid my head on his chest. His skin was silky and brown and smelt of nice shower gel. He was with *me*, not riding or anything else country estate-ish, and being nice to me alone, *not* the world at large. He was being the Jonty I loved again, for the time being. 'Love you,' I said.

'Me too,' said Jonty, twisting a strand of my hair round his fingers.

Some time later we came out squinting into the sun. Jonty had suddenly remembered that Jill was also doing a barbecue lunch for us all, including Christopher and Toby, because she'd been over at Granny's cottage.

'That seems incredibly nice of her,' I said.

'Well, Ma finances her quite a bit, so she likes to repay her in various ways. And, as you've probably noticed, Mum's a lousy cook. And hey, it's a lovely day.' He looked adoringly down at me. 'Isn't it?'

'Sure is,' I agreed. 'Your T-shirt's covered in dove poo.'

'And you think I care?' He swung our clasped hands.

I was happy, very happy. I actually thought, 'I am happy right now – I must remember exactly how it feels.'

The smell of barbecuing drifted towards us. Jill had set up a table on the grass by the door near the kitchen. Gina was there with Christopher and Toby. No sign yet of Flavia and Gil.

'We've been with the horses,' lied Jonty. 'Better wash before we eat.' He hustled me indoors before I had time to take in Jill and Toby, let alone Christopher. 'I think you look great – kind of wild and mussed up, but maybe you'd better go and check in a mirror. You might want to tidy yourself up a bit.' He squeezed my hand. 'And I don't want to be there when the Flavour turns up – she won't corroborate our story about being with the horses.'

'No one will mind, will they? That we've been messing around in the dovecote?'

'Nah. Don't suppose so. Just don't want comments. See you out there toot sweet.'

'See ya.'

I was a mess. My hair was all tangly and my clothes were covered in grot from the floor of the dovecote. I also had a mark or two on my neck. Oops. Luckily I had a similar (clean) pair of shorts and I put on a longer top. I brushed my hair out and arranged it carefully. There. I'd just had a wash and brush up before lunch. Don't know why I cared what they all thought. What did they expect me and Jonty to do? But aagh! Christopher was there, and his little brother with the curls-like-Christopher-used-to-have. And the feminist artist! I found myself hitting the mascara and just the teeniest bit of lipstick. Yes? No? This was daft. I don't fancy Christopher in the slightest. It's just – after what Jonty said. Nah. Jonty probably had his own agenda for saying all that. Something to do with Tamara perhaps. Don't want to think about her. Damn! Why did I have to start thinking about her? Just don't, Holly. Just don't. It'll make me feel all bitter about tonight, and I thought I'd forgotten. Go downstairs, Holly. Sort out the barbecue first.

The barbecue was brick-built into a wall and there was a long garden table with benches and a parasol. Jill had knocked up salads and sauces as well as kebabs and chicken. Gina introduced me to Jill as if I was one of her own friends. I liked that. 'Meet Holly,' she said, 'from London. Holly is a young woman with a mind of her own, unlike so many others I could mention.' I blushed, hoping it was intended as a compliment. I looked at Jill appraisingly. She had wild curly grey hair and vivid blue eyes. She looked brown, as if she spent a lot of time in the garden. She wore some large blue glass beads (exactly the same colour as her eyes), blue denim jeans, a man's white shirt and espadrilles.

'Hi Holly,' said Jill. 'I've heard a lot about you.' That was worrying. Now I knew why Christopher had cringed when I said the same thing to him.

Toby pushed in and shook my hand in a very grown-up way. He must be about the same age as Abby. He said 'Hi!' and then turned to Christopher. 'OK, Chris, you win. She does look like Andie McDowell only prettier.'

'All right, Toby, I think we'll do without the personal comments,' Jill said briskly.

'And you're a real Babe yourself,' I said to Toby.

'Oh, thanks,' he mumbled.

'You've seen the film, of course,' said Jonty.

'Should have been ready for that one, Tobe! Thanks, guys,' said Jill. 'We do our best to squash him, don't we Chris? But we rarely succeed.' Chris was doing manly things to the barbecue and didn't respond. Flavia and Gil turned up then. True to form, Flavia didn't even acknowledge Jill, but sat at the table and grabbed a couple of cold beers for herself and Gil.

'Is Pa coming?' Jonty asked Gina.

'A bit later,' she said. 'Probably just as we're finishing.'

'Well, we're ready to roll now,' said Jill. 'Chris has put the chicken out, and some of the kebabs are ready. Come and help yourselves, everyone.'

We scoffed the lot. I was feeling content despite the ball fiasco. Jonty sat close by and fiddled with my hair or stroked my hand which reminded me all over again of the dovecote and made me smile. Flavia and Gil had been silenced by food. Toby and Chris cleared off to play tennis. I couldn't possibly have been so energetic after a meal in that heat, but nothing seemed to stop them. Jill started to clear up but Gina brought out coffee and stopped her. The six of us were sitting round the table drinking it when Brian turned up.

'No food for a hard-working man, then?' He sounded genuinely peeved.

'Hard work, was it?' Gina asked.

'Well, you know what these meetings are like. And they never give you food, just inferior instant coffee. This looks nicer.' He pulled the cafetière towards him.

'I'll fetch you a cup,' said Jill, getting up before Gina could stop her.

Brian sat down and looked round at us. 'Bet you've all had a better morning than me.'

'Yah,' said Flavia.

'At least we're keeping the horses fit,' said Gil. 'I don't believe for a minute that they can really ban us.'

'What's all this about, Jonty?' I whispered.

'You don't want to know,' Jonty whispered back, but Brian had heard me.

'What's it all about? I'll tell you what it's all about! It's about damn-fool politicians in London thinking they can alter the way we've lived for centuries. They think they have the right to pass legislation on anything at all, never mind that they don't understand the first thing about rural matters, simply because some pressure group or other have decided that it's cruel. Oh, they eat meat, wear leather, use cosmetics – drink *milk*, eat *eggs*, for goodness sake and there's a thing – and think they can make *laws* about what is and what isn't cruel down here in the country.' The normally placid Brian was getting quite red in the face.

It dawned on me that they were talking about hunting. *I* think hunting is cruel and disgusting. I could feel my heart beginning to thump.

Gil joined in. 'No more than you'd expect, is it Brian? I mean, these sentimental prats haven't got a clue have they?'

'Don't see the harm in riding to hounds,' wheedled Flavia.

'It makes my blood boil,' said Brian. 'Where's their sense of beauty? And history?'

'It would be a shame if all the old traditions disappeared,' Gina joined in. 'There's nothing quite like the sight of the hunt going by.'

I was huffing and puffing. Jonty gripped my hand. He has a natural instinct for danger, that boy.

'Never mind how it looks,' said Gil. 'What can beat closing in for the kill? That moment when you know you've *got* the beggar!'

'Well, personally I prefer shooting,' said Gina. 'But that's only because I like to do the business myself and eat what I kill.'

'You've got a point there, Ma,' said Flavia. 'But Grandfather never lets me come on a shoot when we're staying.'

'That's because the Hayters know that shooting is for the men,' said Brian.

'Really Brian!' said Gina. 'In my family we don't leave everything to the men. I've always encouraged my girls to get out there.'

'More's the pity,' grumbled Brian.

I couldn't believe what I was hearing. I tried to think of an innocent sounding question that would expose them all for the bloodthirsty dimwits they undoubtedly were. I smiled but my lip was wobbling. I ignored Jonty's restraining hand. 'So what harm have foxes ever done you?' That would stall 'em.

Wrong question. 'Oh, only ravaged a few tens of newborn lambs and decimated a hen house or five,' said Gina, suddenly defensive and icy. 'And of course they don't eat what they kill – just maim and tear a few heads off and innards out. Nothing much.'

'They're animals,' I said staunchly. 'They don't know any better. But then, hunting's all about behaving like animals, isn't it? Stupid, stuck-up animals, who also don't know any better. Thinking that hurtling around on horseback after a poor defenceless fox, chasing it until it's exhausted and then watching the hounds ripping it apart is *fun!*' I wished I had Zoe on hand to be eloquent for me but *my* blood was boiling now. All the hurt about the ball, the arrogance, Jonty and Tamara, horrible Flavia, made me see red. I didn't care what I said.

Gina tried to placate me, but it was too late. I turned on her. 'What is it with all of you,' I yelled. 'You're all just so sure that you're *right*. Well, you're not!'

'Holly!' said Jonty desperately. 'Please, don't. You simply don't understand . . .'

I brushed him aside and started marching towards the house. 'Enjoy your silly ball,' I said. 'I don't give a stuff. Why should I want to spend my evening with a load of braying hooray Henrys anyway!'

'Holly!'

'Oh leave her, Jonathan,' I heard Flavia saying as I pushed past a questioning Jill.

I vaguely heard Gina telling Jonty that they hadn't meant to upset me, but I was too angry to care as I stormed up to my room and flung myself down on the bed in floods of tears.

I suppose I'd half hoped Jonty would follow me. But he didn't. After ten minutes of hysterical crying I sat up and took stock. Daisy's beautiful ballgown hanging on the back of the wardrobe door didn't help. I started feeling sorry for myself and cried all over again. Still no Jonty. I reached for my diary.

Thursday afternoon
I really have blown it this time. Just when Jonty and I were really getting the hang of being boyfriend and girlfriend, just when he could make me go weak at the knees with a glance – I have to go and ruin everything by blowing my top and being rude and ungracious.

Well, it's all their stupid fault. They don't understand anything normal. How can they kill foxes and shoot beautiful birds for sport? I hate them and everything they stand for. Sorry, Jonty, but that's the way it is. What am I doing here anyway? And how dare they offer me a ball – a BALL for God's sake, and put me and my family to all the trouble of finding a ballgown – and then just withdraw the offer? Where do they get off? The unbelievable arrogance!

I sat for a few moments and gazed out of the window at the beautiful grounds bathed in afternoon sunlight. It must be about four. The barbecue had started quite late. The trees outside my window rustled in the breeze and leaf shadow patterns danced on my floor. It was soothing. I opened the window wider and leaned out. The Hayters were all round the corner – I could hear talking but no words. Late summer scents of cut corn and distant bonfires drifted in.

I felt cut off. Cut off from my own familiar world of London streets and privet hedges and the lido, our strip of London garden, litter, booming cars . . . I thought about Mum and Dad and Abby, and the tears came to my eyes again. I was homesick, goddammit!

I've just discovered homesickness! And naming it makes it feel a little less bad, though I'd give anything to be beamed back home right away and not have to face any Hayters ever again. Even Jonty seems like someone who happened in a dream. As it is, I suppose I'll have to apologise. Ask if I can use a phone to get Mum or Dad to come and fetch me. I'm sure the H's will all be glad to see the back of me.

Wallowing in self-pity, I lay back on the bed again. Exhausted, I fell asleep.

Eight

There was a tap on my door. I heard it through my dreams. There it was again, louder.

'Holly? Holly, can I come in? It's me, Jonty.'

'Hnnurfokay.'

The sun had moved round and my room was dim. 'I came to say that I've got to leave now. And Hol, I'm really sorry. You just don't get on to the subject of hunting with my family. I should have warned you.'

Of course, Dilly already had warned me. I sat up. Jonty was wearing a tuxedo. He looked fabulous. I was speechless. He leaned over me. He smelt freshly showered and – fabulous. He bent to kiss me, tipped up my chin and looked into my eyes. 'Am I forgiven?'

But before I could pull him to me there was a rude beep from outside. 'Have to go – sorry. Flavia's driving all of us over to the Hiltons. Jill will come and pick you up in about half an hour to take you over to Granny's. As I said, you'll have a better evening than me. Bye! Must fly! Princess Tamara awaits!'

He shouldn't have said that. It conjured up a picture of skinny Tamara in a ball gown lying back rapturously and waiting for *my* Jont. Just when I was beginning to think I could forgive at least *him* amongst the hated Hayters.

Jonty was gone. They were all gone. And Jill was going to take me to see a strange Grandmother I'd never even met. She was bound to be just as bad as the rest of them. A woman who could terrorise Tuscany.

I went into my bathroom for the quickest of showers, appreciating the luxury all the more since I was leaving as soon as possible. I changed again into jeans and a clean top under a blouse. I pulled my grubby old hair back into a ponytail and then remembered the marks on my neck and thought better of it.

I could hear the doorbell jangling in the distance. There was a key in the lock and then Jill calling, 'Holly? Are you ready to come to Dorothy's? She's expecting us.'

I ran along the corridor and down the stairs to Jill. I didn't want *her* thinking I had no manners. 'Thank you for picking me up.'

'No problem! I had to fetch some things for Dorothy anyway. Are you all right? Christopher said he thought you'd been upset. I know it's hard, Holly, but don't let these wonderfully archaic people get you down. Accept them for the marvellous eccentrics they are. It's not always the values that count – families like the Cler-mont-Hayters can't really help those. But your Jonty and his mum are both generous and warm people. Gina's my friend. She wouldn't want to upset you.'

We got into her car, a tatty Deux Chevaux. A large potted plant took up the whole of the back seat.

'I feel a bit awkward about spending the evening with an old lady I don't know,' I said.

'Treat it as an experience,' said Jill, smiling. 'Believe me, an evening with Dorothy won't be a hardship. I'll call by again during the evening, and if you're fed up you can either come back with me and the boys or I'll drop you back at the Chase.' We had arrived.

Granny/Dorothy's house was like one of the follies. I hadn't seen it on my tour of the grounds because it was so hidden away. Jill drove into the drive and together we went up to the deep pink front door, Jill clutching the pot plant. The door opened as we approached and an elegant, white-haired, suntanned, upright elderly lady greeted us. She was obviously Gina's mother, but less horsy to look at.

'Come in, come in both of you. I've laid the table on the veranda and the antipasto and the wine are all waiting for us. I hope you'll have a glass of wine with us Holly. A little never did anybody any harm, did it Jill?'

'Thank you,' I said and followed the two of them through Dorothy's extraordinary house. Several surpris-ingly big rooms were connected with little flights of stairs up and down. The walls were white and hung with huge, strange paintings of pink hills, some with little reddish towers on them, others with strange brown or black forests and peculiar little lakes and caves. I'd never seen anything like them before. They were strikingly beautiful. I stopped in front of a pinky-brown landscape with deep clefts and valleys and a golden-brown thicket of trees.

'She's a genius, isn't she?' said Dorothy. 'Dear old Brian can't cope with them in the Chase, so I have the ones Gina's bought as well – not that I mind.'

A flush crept up my neck. *Feminist paintings*. These were Jill's paintings. And they weren't landscapes – as such. They were nudes. Thank goodness I hadn't said anything.

'We'll talk about my Tuscan buyers later, Jill,' said Dorothy. 'Suffice to say that I know I've got definite commitment on at least four of them. Your Christopher's wheeze of putting them on the website worked. Now they can't wait to come and see them. Isn't technology wonderful – don't you think, Holly? Are you *au fait* with the Internet?'

'Yes, Dad lets me use it on his computer for my homework,' I said. 'We want to get a scanner too. I'd never thought of selling art that way. I suppose it makes sense.'

'With an international star like Jill here, yes.'

'Don't make me blush,' said Jill, blushing. 'I don't think I'd be relying on yours and Gina's kind patronage if I was really an international star. But it's nice to know that everything's in place if I suddenly become one. I can't quite imagine it somehow.'

'No such word as "can't", Jill,' said Dorothy. (Just as Dilly had predicted!) We were out on the veranda which ran along the back of the house. It looked out over the garden. There was an outdoor table laid with little dishes of Italian food, three wine glasses and a bottle of wine.

'Just these little bits for me, Dorothy,' said Jill. 'I have to get back to the boys in a minute.'

'Good,' said Dorothy with a smile. 'Then I can have

Holly all to myself. And there'll be all the more pasta for us. It's fresh, you know, Holly. I bought it in Italy this morning. Isn't that incredible?'

I sat down and helped myself to olives, which I *love*, three different sorts. It all seemed very sophisticated. Dorothy poured a little wine into my glass. She lit nightlights in a couple of lanterns. It was lovely. Jonty was right. I was having a nice time. I kind of hoped he *wasn't*. Jill drained her glass of wine, crammed a couple more artichoke hearts into her mouth and stood up. 'OK, I'm off. I have to go and get supper but I'll call by later, Holly. Bye! See you!' And I was on my own with Dorothy.

'I'll just go and put the pasta on, dear,' said Dorothy. 'It's fresh, so it will only take three minutes. You sit back and enjoy the garden. Have a little more wine if you want, but I don't want Gina accusing me of getting you drunk. I have the same arrangement with Cordelia.'

I sat back and relaxed. Wow. Dorothy was something else. Some granny! I liked the way she treated me like a grown-up, a bit like Gina in a way (except I'd blown it with Gina, hadn't I?), as if she didn't know how to be a motherly – or grandmotherly – sort of person. The garden was quiet and gorgeous. The sun was setting. It was all rather romantic. The perfect setting for a fuschia pink ballgown in fact. I was just starting to feel *bitter* again when Dorothy returned with a dish of pasta and a bowl of salad.

She put them down on the table between us. 'There we are dear. Pasta (she pronounced it "parsta") and pesto straight from Tuscany. And salad from Jill's garden. What could be nicer?' She started to serve it out.

I was about to say 'Nothing could be nicer,' but it kind of stuck in my throat. We ate.

'I like to eat early,' said Dorothy. 'Then there's a lot of evening left. Evening is the best time of day for me. Evenings should be devoted to relaxation and pleasure!' She sat back and drank her wine. Then she regarded me over the rim of her wineglass. 'I think you're not speaking your mind Holly. You can, you know. I have an inkling that all is not well.'

(Yeah – that I've been hideously rude and ungracious to my hosts.)

'Have you ever stayed away from home before?'

I thought. 'I've been on school trips. And I've stayed with friends. But mostly I've been away with my family.'

'And you go to a day school, I gather.'

'I would hate to go to boarding-school.'

'Would you? I adored it. Still, no one should have to live away from home until they're ready. There's a time for everything. But I think it's good to stay with another family once in a while – if only to reassure you that yours is the best.'

'I – I wouldn't say that.' I didn't want to be cornered into saying anything bad about the Hayters. Not by their grandmother!

'Of course they are, dear. Everybody's family is the best. And so it should be! Now, Jill left me a summer pudding. Would you be an angel and fetch it from the kitchen? Everything's there on a tray.'

The kitchen was painted in mellow Tuscan colours (I imagined) – deep blue and rose – and mercifully free of Jill's paintings. I carried the tray into the garden. 'I like your kitchen, Dorothy. It feels Italian.'

'It's meant to. Some of my house doubles as an art gallery, but not the kitchen! I don't cook – not worth it for one. But I eat like they do on the continent. Simple food, best quality ingredients. And of course I can knock up pasta and salad like the best of them. More than can be said for my daughter, but she hasn't had the freedom I've enjoyed.'

We ate the summer pudding with thick cream. It was divine. When we'd finished Dorothy made a little pot of espresso and brought it out onto the veranda. She sat down and looked at her watch. 'There. It's only seven-thirty and we have the whole evening ahead of us.' She sighed with pleasure but I couldn't think of anything to say. I couldn't forget the ballgown on the back of the door and Jonty in his evening gear dancing the night away with Tamara.

Dorothy looked over at me. She said tentatively – 'So that silly granddaughter of mine gave the Hilton girl your ticket for the ball, did she?' (Obviously she knew the whole story.)

'Well, the Hiltons are her friends. Jonty said I wasn't missing anything.'

'All very well for him!' said Dorothy. 'Were you looking forward to it *very* much, dear?'

'It's just that I've never been to one before. And we had to go to a lot of trouble to borrow a ballgown, you see. We were going to try and make me one, but there wasn't time.'

'Oh goodness. What a mercy you didn't!'

'Never mind. I *can't* go and that's that.'

Oops. I'd said the magic word. The word that couldn't fail to trigger Dorothy into action.

'*Can't*?' She scraped back her chair and stood up. 'There's no such word! You *shall* go to the ball, if that's what you want! I'd *love* to play fairy godmother.'

'I – I—' Oh blimey. What was she planning? She was drumming her fingers on the table.

'Now, let me think. It's the polo club, isn't it? Goodness, that's just old Felicity doo-dah. I can speak to her. She won't actually go to the ball until it's over, when her Freddie makes the speeches. Hmmm. What's her number?'

'Please, Dorothy – I – I mean Jonty's there with Tamara now. I wouldn't have a partner. And he might not want me there.'

'Nonsense. Anyway, I've thought of that. There's Christopher. It's high time he did something other than play tennis. Pass me my mobile, would you dear?' Aagh. Poor Christopher.

I passed it to her reluctantly. I felt both gloomy and excited, if that's possible. I was almost positive this was going to be a fiasco.

'Jill? Dorothy. Poor Holly feels like Cinderella here, and I thought I'd play fairy godmother. What's Chris up to? He'd be up for a ball, wouldn't he? Has he got the outfit? I've still got Charlie's here, somewhere. Could you pick up Holly's dress? Oh, all right – you come here, pick up Holly and the penguin suit for Christopher, take them both to the Chase to change and then drive them on. That's fine. I'll phone Felicity now.'

I couldn't bear to listen. 'Just going to the loo,' I mouthed, and tiptoed indoors, under the gaze – or whatever – of Jill's nudes, to find one. I already had a nervous stomach ache. I sat on the loo and thought. I had the dress. Shoes weren't too good. Trainers, some Birkenstock-style sandals and another pair of flat sandals from Greece. They'd have to do. I needed to do something about my armpits (major problem with dark hair). They were a bit stubbly for a fancy frock. My legs were OK. Would there be time to wash my hair? I looked at my watch. It was 7.45 already. Probably not. Jill had to get here and *then* drive us to the Chase and *then* we had to change and *then* drive over – we wouldn't be there before nine even if we hurried. I finished and wandered back to Dorothy, still thinking. What about jewellery? What about my hair? I should have had all afternoon to prepare for this, dammit.

Dorothy greeted me with a smile. 'That's all settled then. There will be a pair of tickets with your names on, waiting at the entrance. Just help me carry our plates into the kitchen and Jill will be here before we know.'

She was right. Jill arrived in no time at all. Christopher was with her and so was Toby. Christopher was silent as usual and white as a sheet. He wouldn't look at me. Toby was the opposite. 'It's me you should have asked, Holly. I'm a wicked dancer. Christopher can't dance to save his life.'

'Shut up, Toby,' said Jill. 'Course he can, Holly. Very light on his toes is our Chris.' Christopher's face was like thunder. He was clearly deeply embarrassed. Oooh, this was getting awful. I could have enjoyed a nice quiet evening with Dorothy, watched a bit of TV and then gone back to the Chase to bed. But no. I had to go and open my big mouth. I just had to let on that I was miffed.

'Run up to Charlie's old room, Christopher,' said Dorothy. 'It's all right, it's not haunted – Charlie is happily playing on that golf course in the sky, dear. Look in the closet and you'll see the DJ straight away. There's a bow tie there and a cummerbund too.'

Christopher couldn't escape quickly enough. 'But I'm not sure about a shirt,' Dorothy muttered.

'Never mind,' said Jill, 'I'm sure we can nick one of Jonty's at the Chase.'

'My dear!' Dorothy pretended to be shocked.

Christopher came down with the suit over his arm. It was still wrapped in polythene from the dry cleaners. 'I had everything cleaned before giving it to Oxfam,' said Dorothy (I didn't think the Hayters had heard of Oxfam). 'But then I couldn't bring myself to give some things away. Jonathan might grow into them one day. Or you, Christopher! I think that suit will fit you perfectly. Just try the jacket on, do, before you go off. For my sake.'

Still silent, Christopher slid the jacket out from under the polythene. It was a very posh one. He put it on over his T-shirt. Dorothy was right, it fitted beautifully round his shoulders and back. Hmmm. He looked *rather* tasty in it – apart from the scowl!

'Wow,' said Jill. 'Very dashing, Chris. We should dress you up more often. You were pretty as a girl when you were little – and I always encouraged you to wear bright colours – but you don't half look good in a suit!'

'You'd better get a wriggle on,' said Dorothy. She was clearly loving this. 'I'm afraid I'm too tired after travelling and I've drunk too many glasses of wine to follow later, but I shall want to hear all about it, Holly. Now run along and enjoy yourselves.'

'Thank you so much for making it possible, Dorothy,' I said, beginning to wish she hadn't.

'Glad to be able to wave my magic wand,' said Dorothy. 'And thank you for keeping me company. I'll try and hang on to you for a little longer next time!' She waved us off.

Christopher kept his head down and went to sit in the front seat of their car, leaving me to scramble into the back with Toby. 'That's not very polite to Holly,' said Jill, but Christopher was past caring. Oh great.

We skidded over the gravel and piled out of the

Citroen. 'Use the downstairs shower room, Chris, like you usually do,' said Jill. 'Can you be ready in ten minutes, Holly? I know it's a lot to ask of a girl, but we don't want to turn up there just as it's winding down.' I set off up the stairs. 'Come on Tobes. Grab a coke if you want and we'll watch TV.'

I shut the door of my room behind me and sat on the bed to gather my thoughts. The dress hung invitingly on the wardrobe door. I tried to convince myself that the evening ahead could be fun. It would be if Christopher cheered up – and if Jonty was OK about us turning up and if the other Hayters didn't spoil it in some way. Not much to ask, really. Huh!

I went into the bathroom and stripped off. I tipped my head up and brushed my hair vigorously. I sprayed it with Happy. I held it up on top of my head and then saw the state of my neck. I'd have to wear it down. So I made a few little plaits – I could tie them back to look pretty. I had the quickest of showers and then stood in front of the mirror over the basin to attack my armpits. The razor had seen better days. Ouch. Damn. Blood everywhere. I didn't have another one. Jonty would have one. We were the only people in the house and I was the only one upstairs so I boldly wrapped my towel round me and went down the corridor to Jonty's room. He didn't have a whole bathroom like mine, but he did have his own washbasin and he did shave – sometimes. I went in. His wardrobe was open and the whole room was a mess of Playstation stuff and plastic aeroplanes and computer magazines. There was a photo of us together in Barbados by his bed. I was tempted to root around a bit with him not there, but a razor was the thing. Ha! And there was a whole packet of disposable ones above the basin. And some proper shaving cream. I decided to have another go at my armpits then and there. I tucked the towel firmly round me, ran a basin of hot water, squidged out some shaving cream and tried not to cut myself any more. Ouch again. My armpit was spurting blood. I lifted my arm and leant right towards the mirror to inspect the damage, tongue caught between my teeth in concentration. And then, in the mirror, I saw someone come in. Oh my God. It was Christopher. But he didn't rush out again. He froze. Of all the times to choose.

'I was looking for a shirt,' he said lamely.

'Obviously,' I said, since he was wearing the whole outfit (apart from the DJ), including braces, bow tie dangling round his neck, and cummerbund, without one. 'Carry on. Don't mind me,' I said, also lamely.

Then he looked at me properly – me in a shower cap, neck dotted with purple marks turning green, wrapped in a bath towel, froth and blood oozing out from under my arms. 'Ooh, you're bleeding,' he said.

'Cut myself shaving.' I tried to catch his eye.

And then, he pointed to his chin. 'So've I!' he said, and quite unexpectedly gave a loud hoot of laughter. 'Bloody useless at being posh, aren't we Holly!' He sat down on Jonty's bed in his shirtless outfit and laughed until the tears ran down his cheeks.

I wanted to be cross and say 'Less of the "we"; you speak for yourself!' but he was so hysterical with giggles I couldn't bring myself to. I sat down next to him and laughed too. Then I asked, 'Why was it you came in? Other than to spy on a lady at her toilet, that is?'

'*Toilette!*' he was still chortling. 'A lady at her *toilette* if we're being *poshe*. I didn't reckon on finding you in Jont's room. I was looking for a shirt, as I said.' This was more words than he'd spoken to me the whole time I'd been here. It was more of a transformation scene than any in Cinderella. And then he carried on! 'This outfit hasn't got one – as you can see – and I need a nice white shirt, preferably with pleats and frills, to go with the bow tie and cummerbund. Honestly Holly, I think all this dressing up stuff is complete poo—'

'Oooh, poo-ooh!' I said in a silly voice. I stood up. 'Now stop moaning, Chris. Granny Dorothy has ordained that I shall go to the ball and you're bloomin' taking me. So let's find a shirt.'

Well, we looked through all Jonty's wardrobe and then through his drawers, but not a white shirt was there to be found. Then Christopher pounced on one that Jonty had bought in Barbados. It was a 'tropical' shirt, red, covered in yellow bananas. 'Banana!' I yelled. Christopher looked at me blankly. 'Sorry. Silly game we played in Barbados. Every time you see a banana you shout "Banana".' I trailed off.

'Obviously you had to be there,' said Christopher. And then, 'I like you calling me Chris. Not many people here do.' He held up the shirt and gave an evil grin. 'I'm going to wear this. Let's see how many people say something.'

I wasn't sure. What about me in my fuchsia silk ballgown? Did I want to be with someone in a tropical shirt with bananas on it? Chris was putting it on. 'Help me with the bow tie,' he said. 'It's got a clip at the back.'

'Sit down, then. You're far too tall for me to reach. There.' I clipped it on. He stood up for me to admire the effect. Actually, his tennis-player's body would have looked good in anything, I realised. Yup, it looked good in the gear, even the silly shirt. 'Try it with the DJ.'

There was a clattering of claws along the corridor. The three spaniels had come to look for us, followed by Jill's voice. 'I hope you two are ready. We should have left five minutes ago. Do either of you need a hand?'

'We're fine, Mum. Down in a minute. Go and get your dress on, Holly. I'll wait outside your door and keep Mum posted.'

I scuttled along the corridor. I didn't really want Jill, or Toby for that matter, knowing that I'd been consorting with Christopher dressed only in a bath towel. I whizzed under the shower again, put on some underwear and the Greek sandals and stepped into the dress. Fabuloso! I felt pretty princessy, I can tell you. I couldn't do it up but I whacked on some make-up and a little necklace and earrings Josie had bought me in Camden Market. I looked in the mirror. My hair fell satisfactorily over my neck and the little plaits looked partyish enough, except that I only had a towelling hair thing to tie them with. The dress would look great when it was properly zipped up. Oops, no it wouldn't. I couldn't possibly wear it with a bra. Bra off – please don't come in Christopher. Dress on again. Jewellery looked nice against my tan. All in all, not bad for a first ball. I had a sudden repeat lurch of homesickness. Dad should have been waiting out there with his camera ready to take the 'Holl-doll's first ball' piccy for the album. Concentrate Holly. I tried to do the zip up. I struggled but I just couldn't do the last couple of inches.

'Come on!' Jill's voice.

A knock on the door. 'Are you ready Holly?'

Damn. I opened the door. Chris was loitering there. 'Chris? I'm going to have to ask you to do me up. Cliché and all that, but I just can't do it myself.'

'That's cool,' He said. 'No problem. *Ni probleme*. Turn round.' And then he giggled again. I stood there waiting for him to finish the zip, feeling exposed. He did it up –

there was a little pause and then I felt his fingers gently touch my back. Just once. Nothing more. 'There, all done. Wow! That's quite a dress!'

I sensed a hesitation in his voice. 'It is OK isn't it? I mean, it's a ballgown for a ball, isn't it?'

'You look great,' he said, ever so slightly non-committally. We went down the stairs together. There I was *walking down the stairs* of a stately home in a gorgeous ballgown! What a photo-opportunity. Jill and Toby emerged to watch our entrance.

'Wicked!' said Toby.

'I say,' said Jill. 'That's some dress!' She suddenly plucked a few flowers from one of her arrangements. They were exactly the same colour as the silk. 'Corn cockles,' she said. 'No one will miss them. I'll tuck a few into your hairband. There, gorgeous.' She suddenly clocked Chris's shirt. 'Christopher! You're not sending the whole thing up, are you? This is a formal ball – and you know what old Felicity do-dah and her polo club are like.'

'All I could find, Mum.' Chris gave a shrug and a smile.

'At least you've cheered up.'

'I think it's cool,' said Toby. 'Wish I was going. I'd wear a – a wetsuit or something.'

'That's not the attitude at all. Come on, let's at least get there before it ends.'

Well, what a turnaround. Silent old Chris laughing and being friendly. He wasn't lovesick at all – was he? This time Chris let me sit in the front, but I could feel his eyes on my bare back the whole way there.

Nine

Jill dropped us outside the gates. The venue was the Pump Rooms in one of the small towns. It was all very Georgian and Jane Austen. I wish we'd arrived in a carriage and been greeted by torch-carrying footmen, but never mind. Jill shoved us out of the Deux Chevaux onto the street. 'Back at midnight,' she said, laughing. 'They always end very promptly here – caretaker's an ogre. Have fun!' We were on our own.

This was weird. Jonty was in there somewhere, with all the other Hayters plus Tamara. He didn't know I was coming. I was with Christopher. Christopher, who was, Jonty thought, in love with me. Chris who had suddenly untied his tongue. I remembered Dilly's letter – '*Promise me you won't mess with Chris*'. I wasn't, was I? I looked sideways at him. He was shooting his cuffs and wriggling his neck and chin the way blokes do to accommodate the collar and bow tie. He looked nervous and – well, pretty gorgeous really. Why hadn't I noticed before? Was it because I'd seen him laugh for the first time? Or because he'd sided with me – '*We're* no good at being posh?' He didn't seem fazed by seeing me half-dressed. I guess Jill made sure he had a good attitude to women.

Boy, was I confused. My instinct was to take his arm. But Jonty was in there. *My* Jonty. Christopher nodded to me and gestured the way forward with a wave of his hand. 'Shall we?' he said, and crooked his arm for me to take.

But then he spoilt it by saying, 'I'm gonna go in there and get *smashed*.'

'Christopher!'

'Well, what else am I supposed to do? Jont's going to come and take you away – and I'll have two and a half hours until Mum comes to pick us up. The wine is allegedly horrible, but free. I haven't got a tennis match tomorrow.'

'Chris!' We were just outside the entrance.

He turned to me and put his hand over the arm I had tucked into his. 'Yes?'

'I – Perhaps it won't be like that. Jonty's with Tamara.'

'Oh great. So I get to *act* the boyfriend?'

'No – I just meant – Maybe everyone dances with different partners?'

'It's not a school dance, Holly. Jonty's told me the score. You either go with your girlfriend and snog the entire time or you go on the pull. At least, the girls try to and the boys mostly go on the booze. So what's new? It's the same with the toffs as with anyone else.'

We were in. A woman sat at a table. 'Yes?' she said. 'And who are you?'

'You're holding tickets for Miss Holly Davies and Mr Christopher Green,' said Chris.

'Oh, yah,' said the woman, opening an envelope. She fished out the tickets and handed them to a man who looked like a bouncer. We followed him up some steps to a pair of double doors. He threw them open with a flourish. 'Miss Holly Davies and Mr Christopher Green,' he announced – to a room empty except for a skinny figure sprawled in a chair at the back who looked exceptionally like Tamara in a slinky dress. She got up and came over to us where we stood by the doors.

'Oh my God,' she said, with unmistakable malice. 'A meringue. A magenta meringue. That is *so* two years ago!'

I flinched, visibly, I know. I wanted to turn and flee. Chris gripped my wrist protectively. 'Look at *me*, Tamara. You don't think *we* take a polo club bash so seriously, do you? Anyway, where is everyone?'

'Eating,' said Tamara. 'Disgusting. I ate some to please Mother, but I got rid of it. You'd better not let Jonty see you two together. He's been going on all evening about "I wonder what Holly's doing now?" ' (whingey voice). She sighed. 'I wish I hadn't come. I only did it so's I could wear my Donna Karan.'

'Where is Jonty?' I asked.

'Why should I know?'

'Because you came here with him as his partner,' I said, and had to add, 'making it impossible for him to bring me.'

Christopher tugged at my arm. 'She's a waste of space. Holly. Let's go and find the bar.'

'Suit yourselves,' said Tamara, and aimed herself in the direction of the loos. The dance was about to start again.

Without us noticing, the band had slipped back into their seats. They launched into something a bit smoochy. 'For you two alone!' called the bandleader.

'What, us?' I asked.

'There's no one else around,' said Christopher.

'OK, then. Come on,' I said, and pulled him into a waltzy sort of dance.

'OK,' said Chris. 'But just remember, you started it.'

He put his hand on my back, my bare, bra-less back, and interlaced the fingers of his other hand in mine. He pulled me in towards him, so my head was crushed against his banana-clad chest. I've never been taught this sort of dancing, but Christopher led, nudging my leg back with his. He could dance – Toby was lying.

What's more, it was *incredibly* sexy. All this time, and I never realised ballroom dancing was sexy!

'Count!' said Chris. '*Back*, two, three. *Turn*, two, three. *Forward*, two, three. That's it! And again!'

Hey! I was dancing! I could do it! But it was Chris teaching me, not Jonty. And it should have been Jonty. We were still the only two dancing, more or less the only two in the whole room. The band slowed the tempo down. I was getting the hang of it! I kind of forgot who Chris was and just got into the dancing, spinning round the floor in my silk ballgown. But then I was aware of his hand just stroking my back, ever so gently, his fingers reaching up into my hair. I risked peeping up at him. His eyes were shut.

The song came to an end. The room was filling up. We stopped. Christopher seemed to wake up with a jolt. 'Need a drink,' he said gruffly. 'I'll look out for Jonty. See you!' And he disappeared, leaving me in my 'magenta meringue' in a room that was filling up with girls and women in long slinky dresses, short cocktail dresses – strappy little *décolletée* numbers, but not a traditional ballgown between them. *Oh* dear.

I spotted Flavia and Gil. I tried a little wave, but they blanked me. I saw Gina and Brian and ducked. I didn't fancy talking to Gina right now. Chris wasn't coming back, it seemed. Where was Jonty?

I pushed through the dancers towards the room Chris had been heading for. There was a bunch of extremely drunk looking teenagers, my age and a bit older, on seats by the bar. Some of the girls were on the boys' laps – they seemed to have forgotten that they weren't somewhere private. A small group of lads had their backs to me. Christopher was with them and they were all smoking their heads off.

'Hey man, you look *so* cool,' one guy was saying to him.

'Yeah, in my shirt! Why didn't I think of that!' It was Jonty speaking! He sounded uncharacteristically sarcastic.

'So where's your bird?' someone was asking Chris.

'Around, somewhere,' I heard him mumble.

'What about yours, Jont? What have you done with her?'

'Dunno,' said Jonty. 'Don't care, stupid cow.' He sat leaning right over, his head hanging down. He was pretty far gone. Was he talking about me? I stood on the fringe of their circle. I'd known tonight was going to be a fiasco. But this bad? Could it get any worse?

It could.

Chris went right up to Jonty. 'I hope you're not talking about Holly,' he said.

'Why should you care?' said Jonty nastily. 'Oh yes, of course. You fancy her, don't you? Well, hands off, because she's *mine*.'

'So why d'you agree to bring Tamara tonight?' Chris's eyes were blazing. 'You knew Holly wanted to come.'

'Oh – *because*.' Jonty shook his head and took another drag on his cigarette. (He wasn't a very convincing smoker.) 'Sisters, you know. Anyway, Holly didn't mind.'

'She did,' said Chris. 'That's why I've brought her. Your grandmother set it all up.'

Jonty sat up. 'You *what*? Holly's *here*?'

I didn't know what to do. Jonty was wrecked, a mess. At least I wasn't the stupid cow. But Chris was in fighting form. 'Yes, she's here. And she's been dancing with me. You don't deserve her, Jont.'

The other guys were backing off. It looked as though

Christopher and Jonty were spoiling for a fight. Over me.

I was paralysed. Should I go over to Jonty, my boyfriend? Up until an hour ago I hadn't felt anything at all for Chris – had barely exchanged a single word; now I felt we had a bond which I didn't want to betray. What's more, he was stone cold sober. Jonty wasn't.

But then Tamara returned. The dress was to die for, but her face looked terrible. She hadn't sussed out the situation at all. She went up to Jonty. 'I suppose, now *she*'s here, you won't want to be with me any more.'

'Never did in the first place,' said Jonty. He *really* wasn't himself – one of the nice things about Jonty is that he'd never hurt anyone intentionally.

'You can at least give me a cigarette,' said Tamara.

'Help yourself,' said Jonty. Then he spotted me. 'Holly!' he said. 'My gorgeous Holly! You look so – so – '

'Ridiculous,' muttered Tamara.

' – pretty!' said Jonty. He started staggering towards me. 'I just want to—'

I stood frozen to the spot. Chris was beside me, his fists still bunched. Then he suddenly relaxed. He grabbed Jonty by the shoulders. 'Hey, man. Back off. You know what happens next, and you don't want to throw up on Holly.'

'Yes, yes. Sorry, I'm sorry, sorry man.' All the fight had gone out of Jonty and it was now as clear to me as it had been to Chris that he was about to be sick.

'Take him outside, Tamara,' said Chris. 'It's the least you can do.'

I wasn't so sure about this. 'But—'

'Trust me,' said Chris. 'Jont will throw up and then he'll have a nice little sleep and he won't remember anything about it.'

'But he's my boyfriend – I ought to look after him.'

'I think not. Just flatter yourself that he got into that state missing you. Anyway, Tamara's used to people throwing up.' Tamara was guiding Jonty out through the door. She hadn't fussed, despite the Donna Karan. Most of me didn't like it, but a part of me was glad to let her look after him. After all, she'd made him bring her.

I turned to Chris. 'This is a mess, isn't it? What is it people say about wishes? "Don't make them because they might just come true"?'

'Huh,' said Chris, and looked away.

It was foul where we were. Mostly dark and smoky with a few unpleasantly bright spotlights, and sticky underfoot. The people sitting around were oblivious to the rest of the ball. 'What shall we do now?' I asked.

'Well, we could go back in and dance, but I think it's wrinkle-time in there, judging by the music. Or we could grab some crisps and drink and go and sit outside. There are lawns out the back. It's still a nice evening.'

'OK.' (Well, what would *you* have done?) I found an exciting bottle of unopened fizzy mineral water and Chris spotted a whole new tube of Pringles that had rolled onto the floor. 'Lead the way,' I said.

We made our way back towards the dance hall, where french windows opened down the side to a terrace and then, lower down, a lawn. It had been made very pretty with strings of fairy lights and a few outdoor candles stuck into the ground. There weren't many people out there because there was nowhere much to sit. We headed for the steps that led down to the lawn. 'I don't want to dirty Daisy's dress,' I said.

'They had loads of paper napkins in there. I'll get you some.' Chris nipped back inside for a pile of them and made a little seat for me. 'Now you're going to say you're cold, aren't you?'

'Well, now you mention it . . .'

'Have my jacket – Charlie's jacket.' He peeled it off, revealing the banana shirt in its full glory. 'Comfortable?'

'Very.'

We sat in companionable silence for a while. It was almost dark. The flowers in the herbaceous borders glowed in the twilight and the stars were just appearing. My beautiful dress fell in silken folds round my feet. I began not to care that it wasn't quite the right sort of dress, I felt good in it again. I hoped Jonty was all right. I half wished I'd never come, but sitting here with Chris was OK – different, anyway.

'This is really weird, Chris. I can't believe we're sitting here *talking*. You've barely spoken a word to me all week – until tonight.'

'Ah, well, silence is good too, you know. We've just had a very pleasant silence.'

'You know what I mean. Why wouldn't you talk to me those first few days?'

'Oh, just shyness, I expect.'

'I always talk too *much* when I'm feeling shy.'

'Drop it, Holly. You know perfectly well why I was shy. Don't make me say it. I don't want to spoil things for you and Jonty.' He took a swig from the bottle of mineral water.

'I'm scared I've spoilt things for myself with all the Hayters. I was so rude to Gina earlier. I'm completely out of my depth with them, you know. Everything about them, all their – their assumptions – they're just coming from such a different place from me. I think I'm OK – professional parents, nice enough house, just been to

Barbados – but they make me feel like – well, to use your word – poo. Completely insignificant.'

'You wanna talk about the Hayters? OK, we'll talk about the Hayters. But don't forget that Jonty is my mate. Dilly is my mate, and Gina and particularly Dorothy, are my mum's mates. We don't come from the same place at all either, and I dare say our place is a good deal further away than yours, but you have to see things from other people's point of view. That's what Mum's always taught us.'

'Your mum's quite a lady, isn't she? I like her.'

'Mum's cool. She's brilliant at her work – if you like that sort of thing, but not at earning money.'

'What happened to your dad – do you mind me asking?'

'Ah, well, we don't see him. Mum left him when we were babies and he went to Australia. Mum's not that bothered about men. I mean she likes us, but she's an artist first and she doesn't want to have to look after a man or be bossed about by him.'

'You're very cool about it all.'

'Have to be. Anyway – that just happens to be how my family is. Mum doesn't embarrass us beyond the subject of her painting. But I'm proud of her. It would be so excellent if she got the recognition she deserves. That's partly where Gina and Dorothy come in. They buy Mum's paintings at prices they think they're worth. They both know about art and they think it will be worth a lot more one day. But they know it's not enough for Mum to bring us up on, so they pay her to do other things as well —'

'Like flower-arrangements and cooking?'

'Yeah. They're pretty good to us. "Philanthropic" is the word Mum uses.'

'And your Mum doesn't mind?'

'Why should she? It means she can get on with what she wants to do. And they genuinely appreciate the other stuff she does for them. And she likes them. You've met Dorothy – she's great. She and Mum get on really well.'

'Wow. The people I met in Barbados made me feel boring. Now you do too.'

'Believe me, boring is good.'

'I've heard that somewhere before, too. Now I feel even more terrible about mouthing off at Gina. I know she's OK underneath. She was great yesterday when we went to Stratford. She's not like other mothers.'

'There's nothing to stop you apologising to her. Mum's very keen on apologising. She's always losing her rag with people and then ringing up the next day. She says people soon stop minding – and you can sometimes say what you really mean.'

'My mum and dad are the opposite. They always say, "Least said, soonest mended". Trouble is, I get so *angry* sometimes. Especially when I know I'm right.'

'If you ask me, you should probably be brave and apologise to Gina. She likes people speaking their minds. Brian's more – well, deadly dull really. Mum doesn't have a lot of time for him. And Flavia's just appalling. I think they've all given up on her. Don't know what Gil sees in her.'

'Money?'

'Holly! Hope that's not all you see in Jonty?'

'If I did, I'd hold it against him!'

'Wish you'd hold it against m—'

'Don't wish – it might come true.'

'Only joking.' There was another long pause. 'Holly?'

'Yes?'

'Can I tell you something? I'm not sure how to put it – you mustn't get me wrong. I'm not prejudiced – how could I be?'

'What are you on about?'

'I want to tell you something.'

'Go on then.'

'I don't know how to say it without giving other things away, but since nothing's going to come of it anyway, I suppose it doesn't matter.'

'Get on with it.'

'OK. Deep breath. Hang on, I'll have another swig of water.' He tipped up the bottle. 'Right. Here goes.'

'As soon as I saw you, I felt something I'd never felt before. I just fancied you so much I didn't know what to do.'

'This *is* going to make things difficult, Chris—'

'No, hear me out. It was pure lust. Pure lust, Holly! Nothing sweet and innocent at all! Up until then I'd look at girls and wonder if I fancied them. I didn't fancy Flavia – who could, apart from Gil? I love Dilly and she loves me, but there's no chemistry between us. I thought there must be something wrong with me.'

'Dilly adores you,' I said.

'I know,' he said coolly.

'What about the rest of the world? Film stars, models, people in *Neighbours*? School? *Loaded, FHM*? That's what all the boys in my class drool over. Surely you don't base everything on your experiences with the Hayter family, you sad person?'

'Course not. But you don't understand – these things run through my head the entire time. Especially with Dilly, you know. We're close. And I kind of thought things ought to happen, but they didn't.'

'Seems to me that she's more like a sister, anyway.'

'Maybe, but I'm trying to tell you something important Holly.'

'That you're a normal guy. Big deal.' I knew it was unfair of me, but I suppose I'd kind of been hoping for a declaration of undying love.

'It's more than that Holly, and you know it, but what's the point in making it worse if you're going out with Jonty? I could say, "Oh they're miserable upper-class twits, the lot of them. Forget him and go out with me." But I don't think that. Jont's my best mate. You're his girlfriend. Best friend's girlfriend – big no-no. End of story.'

'I love that film, don't you?' I said. 'I just love the ending when Louis Armstrong says "end of story"!' I waved my arms around, and the jacket slipped off my shoulders.

'End of story is *not* a concept I love, no.' He turned to me. 'Put the jacket back on, Holly. I might not be responsible for my actions if you expose your flesh to me any more tonight, I behaved very well in Jonty's room, didn't I?'

'I suppose you did. I assumed it was because the flesh on view was mixed up with shaving foam and blood – *very* seductive.'

'I'm used to all *that*. Mum's not a great one for shutting the bathroom door. See what I have to put up with? She doesn't want me putting women on a pedestal. Trouble is, she knows me too well. She knew straight away how I felt about you.'

'Mothers are like that.'

'Anyway, I meant when you asked me to do your zip up.'

I remembered the pause after he'd done it up and then the touch of his fingers, and I realised as if I'd seen it that he'd kissed them and planted the kiss on my back. 'OK, you behaved very well.'

Chris suddenly stood up. 'I think I'm going to find some alcohol.'

'You said that before.' I stood up too. This conversation had been so inconclusive. Was he trying to tell me that he was actually in love with me? What did it make me feel about Jonty? I didn't want to be left alone. There was no one near us. All the noise was coming from inside. It sounded as though someone was giving a speech. I wondered what the time was, but I didn't have my watch on. It must be nearly midnight. I reached tentatively for Chris's wrist and the jacket fell off again.

My hand touching his arm changed everything. It was like a flash of electricity. Chris turned on his heel and pulled me to him. He bent and kissed my shoulders and before I knew it he was kissing me on the mouth. Serious kissing, the sort I'd only just learned with Jonty. But it came from me as much as from him. There was a burst of clapping from the hall (kind of appropriate), but a few seconds – or a few light years – later we heard voices coming down from the terrace towards us.

'You'd better not have lost it, Tamara.'

'Well you shouldn't have lent them, Bea, if you cared that much,' Tamara wailed. 'We were standing about there, where that couple are *eating* each other. Jonty made a pass at me and—'

'What's the matter? Do you know them or something?'

'Come on, Bea. You couldn't mistake *those* clothes, could you?'

Chris asked Jill to whizz me back to the Chase and let me in in the hope that I could simply creep upstairs to bed. He pretended I'd had too much of the vile wine. I left my sandals at the bottom of the stairs so they would know I was in and shot up to my room. I was terrified of meeting any of them, but I heard them all come in later, so that at least was lucky.

Diary, I needed my diary. I turned off the light in my bedroom and sat in the bathroom with just the shaving light on. I didn't want anyone thinking I was awake and knocking on my door.

Thursday night/Friday small hours
Aaaagh! Complicated *day! Seems to have gone on for ever. I'll go through it bit by bit. Maybe find some sense in it all.*

1. Woke up all excited about Daisy's ballgown (if only I'd known). Then Flavia, such a sweetheart, told me I wasn't invited and Jonty told me I'd have a better evening at his Granny's. Kuh! (But how right he was!)

2. The dovecote interlude. Hmm. Possibly I'm becoming a bit of a slag in my old age. Anyway, I have to remember that it's great with Jonty. It's nice that he hasn't had a proper girlfriend before and I haven't had a boyfriend – we kind of make it up as we go along (hope no one reads this). Then we had to stop (probably a good thing) because Jonty remembered

3. the lunchtime barbecue. Saw Jill for the first time. She's amazing. The most alive *woman I've ever met. Chris still silent at this point. (Perhaps it would have been better if he'd never opened his mouth – see later!)*

4. The part I'd rather forget. See last entry. No excuses really. I acted like a four-year-old. I will have to apologise tomorrow. Think I know what to say now.

5. Dorothy, and Jill's paintings. Interesting. More later.

6. And then CHRIS. I don't know what I've done. Dilly told me not to mess with him, and I have. I kind of led him on. I think. He told me all this amazing stuff about his family. It was all so intense – there was this incredible tension between us building up all evening. And then we had this kiss that went on and on for ever and set off all sorts of fireworks inside me. I felt completely 'ravaged' (tho' I'm not quite sure what that means).

Right Holly. I have to get my head round this somehow. Tomorrow is Friday and then Saturday is my last day, assuming they don't send me home for bad behaviour! I need never see Chris again, though God knows, I want to. I could go home tomorrow and never see any of them again. I could sneak down and ring Mum and Dad now. But I know what they'd say.

Decision time.

Jonty will know by now that Bea and Tamara saw me with Chris, but I know he made a pass at Tamara. I do love Jonty, but compared with the effect Chris had on me – well, perhaps it's a bit mundane. Jonty and I could both say last night was all a terrible mistake and carry on where we left off. Or we could say it's not working, just try to be friends and have a nice last two days. I keep remembering Chris kissing me, and the way he held me. He was just so – passionate, I suppose. As if he'd really kept his feelings bottled up and they were all coming out.

I decided to sleep on it. It was tempting to ring the parents, but they would only tell me it's no use running away from problems.

When I woke up I knew that the first thing I had to get off my chest was apologising to Gina. I'd been worrying about it all through the night. At seven o'clock I got up, showered and finally washed my hair. Then I dressed and waited by the door for sounds of people going downstairs. I heard Gina and Brian talking, gave them five minutes, took a deep breath and went down. Brian was eating cornflakes in the kitchen. Gina was standing by the kettle.

'Gina,' I came straight out with it. 'I got up early because I wanted to apologise for my behaviour yesterday. I was childish and ungrateful. I hope you'll forgive me.'

'Forget it,' said Gina, peremptorily. 'Cup of tea?'

'Thank you,' I said. I piled loads of sugar into it and quite enjoyed it.

'Granny enjoyed your company very much last night,' said Gina. 'You must see her again before you go. I gather she sent you to the ball?'

'Yes. It was very kind of her.'

'Silly of me not to realise you'd mind. I should have stepped in and not been browbeaten by the terrible Hilton woman.' (Now she was apologising to *me*!) 'I feel rather sorry for poor old Tamara though. Little vixen, but you know she has an eating disorder? And so young.'

'Her mother does seem rather obsessed with food.'

'Exactly. And appearances. And money. He's in business, of course, and hardly ever there.'

Brian looked up, smiling. It seemed he'd forgiven me too. 'Now, now chicken,' he said to Gina. (*Chicken?*) 'Old money you might be, but we all stoop to business these days.'

I didn't know what he was talking about.

'It's Gina's business talent that keeps this place going, you know,' he said proudly.

'I'm sure Holly's not interested, dear,' said Gina. She turned to me again. 'Brian loves to wind me up. I expect Jonathan will be late this morning. I gather he hit the wine rather hard at the bash last night. Still, he has to learn.' (See what I mean about not being the usual motherly type? My parents would have gone ape.) 'I'm glad you're a sensible girl Holly.' (Little did she know.) 'I think he and Tamara have some more riding planned for you for this afternoon – followed by a swim, I dare say. It's a lovely morning. I'd go and sit outside if I was you. There's a pile of magazines in the lobby if you want.'

It seemed like a good idea. I picked up some magazines and took them into the gazebo. Huh! Gina isn't stupid. Well, I knew that, but she doesn't suggest things without a reason. The magazines were *Horse and Hound* and *Tatler* and *Country Life*. And every one of them contained articles on the pros and cons of hunting. I felt compelled to read them. And I learned a lot. Now, I'll *never* approve of killing animals for sport, but I do see that a complete ban on it would change all sorts of aspects of country life, and not just the nice red jackets and steamy breath on the frosty air etc, etc. All the hounds would probably be put down. There would be no more point-to-points. The Pony Club, which is linked to the hunt, wouldn't be able to survive. Other game sports would also have to be banned. Including angling. And my dad *loves* fishing. Face it, Holly, you should have kept your big mouth shut. Oh well, at least I understand the issues better now. I tried to remember what Zoe had said in the school debate on the subject – I know she was all for banning it. Perhaps we should have another one.

I rubbed my arms that were suddenly goosepimply. That bright start to the day had been untrustworthy. Clouds were coming up round the horizon and the trees shivered in the breeze. I felt tired – like you do when you've got up too early. Yesterday had been a funny old day. I went in, putting my head round the kitchen door to tell Gina that I was going to write some letters in my room. She nodded at me over her newspaper. 'I certainly don't expect to see Jonathan or Flavia for a while,' she said. 'I'll tell Jonathan where to find you if he asks.'

'Thanks,' I said, all politeness now. I was grateful to Gina for letting so much water go under the bridge.

In my room I snuggled under the duvet with my diary and tried to marshall my thoughts again. I might have apologised to Gina, but I still had Jonty to sort out. And Chris. Tamara's whingey voice saying 'Jonty made a pass at me' . . . Do you know, I hadn't really registered that statement before – I'd been feeling so guilty about Chris. But now it hit me with its full force. Had Jonty *really* made a pass at Tamara? How *could* he? After our time in the dovecote. But then I'd got off with Chris hadn't I? Though that was different. No it wasn't. Yes it was – Tamara just wasn't fanciable. But then maybe Jonty would think the same about Chris. Nah. I couldn't believe Jonty would have made a pass at Tamara unless he'd been completely out of it. Ooh dear. He had been out of it. Probably, knowing Jonty, he'd just been nice to her. And she'd reckoned that was making a pass. Hmmm.

And I suppose Jonty *would* have been told about me and Chris. Bea. Flavia. Jonty. It was a short route, possibly taking in Gina and Brian along the way. I'd hated them all so much last night I hadn't cared. And I suppose Jill and Dorothy would know by now too. But then I remembered Jill's advice about seeing things from other people's point of view. Gina and Dorothy no doubt regarded adolescent antics from a distance. And what's a kiss at a dance, either way? OK, a lot from my point of view, but not from theirs.

Why is life so difficult? I couldn't really be bothered to write my diary. I'd agonised about most of this stuff last night. A little zizz seemed more appealing. So a little zizz it was.

There was a discreet knock on my door. 'Come in,' I said, swinging my legs over the side of the bed as if I hadn't been asleep. (Why do we always pretend we haven't been asleep? It's the same if I fall asleep babysitting. I always pretend to be wide awake when the parents come home.) It was Gina.

'We've just had a call from Judy Hilton, dear. Apparently Tamara's gone missing. She didn't say anything to you at the do, did she? No funny plans to go off with some boy or anything? I wouldn't want you to tell tales about your friend, but Judy is just a little worried. They think she might have been out all night. She left her mobile behind, which isn't like her.'

I rubbed my eyes, trying to take all this in. My friend? Some boy? There was me thinking they knew everything and hoping they didn't care, but they knew *nothing*! Less than nothing. And, in Judy Hilton's case, hardly seemed to care either. 'Just a little worried'? My parents would have been out of their *minds*!

'What does Jonty think?' I asked. 'I mean, he was with her last night more than I was.'

'Oh, was he dear? I rather thought I saw her trailing round after you and Christopher.'

That one moment. How easy to misread a situation. Then I had a thought. 'Didn't you say she and Jonty were planning a ride?'

'Yes, I did, didn't I? That must have been when we stopped off at Bury on the way.'

'Might she have gone out on her pony? With Jonty even?' I didn't really want to know the answer to this question.

'Not with Jonathan, no. He's still dead to the world. But I'll suggest they check the ponies. Now I come to think of it, she and Jonathan were talking about a ride through the forest. It's tricky in places and Jonathan was wondering if you'd be able to manage.'

Thanks, Jont.

'Can I do anything?' (Not that I was hugely keen to unearth Tamara, you understand.)

'No, no. You carry on with your letter-writing. I'll rouse Jonathan. High time he got up. Maybe he can shine some light on the situation.' She backed out of my room and shut the door, leaving me to my 'letter-writing'. (I'd forgotten about that.)

I got up and looked out of the window. The day had turned nasty. It was wet and unseasonably cold, as it can be when September isn't all that far away, I've noticed. Sharp little reminders that the autumn term starts in just over a week. Huh. No tennis for Chris today then. I suddenly thought of Alex and her tennis tournaments. Maybe Chris has already come across her or some of her ten billion brothers. Quite possibly, I suppose. Oh Chris, Chris. What did I feel about all that stuff last night? How would I feel in two days when I'd said goodbye to both Jonty and Chris?

I wondered if my relationship with Jonty was a bit one-sided. Had I fancied him more than he fancied me? Did I *like* him more than he liked me? A new and worrying thought, that, best tucked away. It really was vile outside. Not a day for a riding picnic.

As if my brain had conjured up the image for itself I spotted Jonty striding across the wet drive in his riding gear plus a navy blue cagoule. I was going to yell down to him, but he looked very purposeful and the trees rustling in the wind made quite a racket to shout over. I wondered where he was going. Could this have anything to do with Tamara? Was he in fact striding purposefully after *Tamara*?

Rrrrahrr! Diary. I needed to vent my spleen.

Friday morning
God I hate Tamara. Unfanciable, did I say? Unappealing,
unattractive. Unlovable? Too right she is! What can Jonty
possibly see in that skinny little zip turned sideways? Blonde
she may be, but her stupid face with her mouth always
hanging open is witchy and ugly. No wonder people bully her.
I would. And she thinks she's so great just because she lives in
a big house and can ride a horse.
Hate Hate Hate.

And I drew a little picture of her on the ground with pointy things sticking out of her and drops of blood.

There. That felt better. I decided not to hide in my room any more. Anyway I felt like a drink. And I was just a teensy bit curious to find out what was going on.

Flavia and Bea were in the kitchen. They were making coffee and ignored me completely. I poured myself some orange juice from the fridge and sat down with

111

the paper. They were tittering and joking about Tamara.
'Stupid kid!' said Flavia, with a snort.

'Drivelly attention-seeking as usual,' said Beatrice.
'Honestly, she'll try anything. Not eating. Eating and throwing up. I don't understand it. She gets whatever she wants. That dress last night cost over a thousand pounds.'

'Hah!' said Flavia. 'What a waste of money!' And they both cackled.

'Come over to mine,' said Bea. 'Mother's doing salmon for lunch because the Page-Joneses are coming over. She's furious already that Tamara isn't there, so she'll be really glad to see you.'

'Page-Joneses?' said Flavia.

'You know. Twin boys. Non-identical. Mother adores them.'

'Oh yah!' Flavia remembered. 'Bags the goodlooking one!'

They went off, still without acknowledging me. I could hear their conversation trailing into the distance. 'That's not fair,' Beatrice was saying. 'You've got Gil!'

I sat there for a while not quite knowing what to do. The older girls had left. Gina was working. Brian was doing whatever he did to fill the day – arranging to massacre another lot of defenceless wild animals probably. I wanted to see Jonty and make sure we were OK – still friends, that is, even if we had both transgressed – though now I wasn't sure any more how much he knew about me and Chris (or whether he had actually transgressed himself). I wanted to see Chris too, but I was scared. Best not to see him alone.

The telephone rang. I looked around stupidly for

someone to answer it, and of course there was no one but me. I picked it up gingerly. 'Hello?' I said tentatively.

'Hol, it's me, Jonty.' He sounded out of breath. 'Look, I'm ringing from a phone box outside the Green Man pub. I've found Tamara's horse. But not Tamara. I think she might have had a fall. I need someone to help me look for her – on horseback. You can't get through the woods quickly on anything else. The ground's really slippery. Is Flavia there? Or Ma?'

'No,' I said. 'Flavia's gone to Bury with Beatrice. You could ring her there.'

'Damn,' said Jonty. 'My money's about to run out. You'll just have to get help Holly. Look – I'll – I'll – ' And the phone went dead.

Help? Me? I was on my own and I didn't know anyone's phone number. I couldn't even ride a horse properly. For some reason I remembered Maddy saying one of her friends had to find a lost child on holiday and how calm she'd been. Unlike me! Help! *I* needed help. All this for toffee-nosed Tamara. Use your *brain*, Holly.

Jonty was outside in the pouring rain by a pub called the Green Man, with two horses. Tamara was possibly lying in a ditch somewhere. (A very small, mean part of me rejoiced.) If Tamara was injured she'd need medical help. Aaaaah. What should I do?

Deep breath. I rang Directory Enquiries and got the number for the Hiltons at Bury. I rang them but amazingly I got the answer service. Could they really not be answering the phone because they were having a lunch party – with Tamara missing? Still, they didn't know she might be injured. They just thought she was seeking attention again.

To be honest, the next call I made was to Mum and Dad. I needed to hear their voices. I got Mum. 'Mum,' I wailed, before she had a chance to chat. 'You've got to help me. There's this girl who's gone missing and she's probably fallen off a horse and it's raining. I'm on my own but I've got to get help for her.' I told her about my call from Jonty.

'Calm down, sweetie,' said Mum in her gorgeous Scottish voice that I was missing like anything. You need to do 999 to alert the emergency services, and you need someone to go out to Jonty with a mobile phone. Surely there are plenty of mobile phones knocking around in that house?'

'I wouldn't know where to look, Mum. The girl who's hurt left hers at her house, but no one is answering there.'

'Is there anyone else you can ring? Friend? House-keeper or something?'

'Of course, Mum. I was so flustered I couldn't think. I don't know where Mrs B. is today. But there's Granny. And there's Jill.'

'Jill sounds possibly more use than Granny.'

'You haven't met this Granny. But you're right. I'll ring Jill. Except I don't know her surname or the name of her house. This is mad. I know. I'll ring Dorothy and then –'

'You've lost me, darling, but I think you should get on. Let me know what happens. Love you loads, byee.'

Directory Enquiries again. Dorothy Clermont, Clermont Lodge. Please don't let her be ex-directory. Amazingly she's not. I rang her.

'Hello dear. I'm resting up in bed today I'm afraid. All that travelling. Jill's number, you say? Of course dear, Jill Green, I know it off by heart. Here you are – I'll ask you about the ball another time.'

Great. Jill would know what to do. The phone rang a

long time. Toby answered. 'Holly!' he said. 'What did you do to my brother last night? I – '

'Toby, this is a bit of an emergency. Is your mum in?'

'I thought you'd be wanting to talk to my brother not my mum.'

'Toby – Can I speak to Jill please?'

'No, you can't. She's not here. But *Chris* is. Shall I get him?'

'I suppose you'd better.'

'I could hear him calling, 'Chri-is! It's for you-ou! Guess who's on the phone!'

Then Chris. 'Holly!'

'Chris – there's a bit of an emergency. I need help.'

'What's up?'

I told him.

'We've got a mobile. Mum's out, though. I'll cycle over. Then we can go over to the stables. Tell you what, meet you over there in ten minutes. You know how to get there, don't you? Maybe one of the lads will be able to help, too. Call 999 and tell them we'll keep in touch. See you.'

I called 999 and spoke to a really nice guy. He said they did have a couple of doctors who rode, but if Tamara was badly injured she might need a helicopter. They were sending someone over to the Green Man. Jonty should have rung them first really. Still, he hadn't known he was going to get a wally like me, had he? Wally Holly.

Enough self-pity. I ran over to the stables, through all those wet nettles and muddier-than-ever molehills. My cross-country run got me there at the same time as Chris who'd ridden down the road on his bike. We were both very wet.

It was lunch time and there were no lads about. 'I'll

take Shakespeare,' said Chris, rooting around in the tack room. (Where were those lads? Nothing was locked. Lucky in some ways). 'Do you want Gorse?'

'Chris – ' I should have foreseen this. 'I – couldn't ride one of those great—'

'Take the bike then,' said Chris, swinging himself up onto the huge dapple-grey. 'Follow me to the Green Man. Then perhaps you can station yourself in the telephone box or something.'

So I got on Chris's bike (large, with crossbar), and followed him out into the lane.

The pub was opposite a bridle path that led into the woods. It was only about fifteen minutes of hard cycling away. Luckily there wasn't much traffic on the roads. I felt very vulnerable following a horse on a bike, and visibility was lousy. An ambulance was already parked in the pub car park. We rode – in our various ways – up to it.

'You the lass that rang us?'

'Yes.'

'No one here seems to be able to tell us anything.'

'I can,' said Chris. 'I think I can piece things together. There's this clearing which we called Foxhole – in the middle of the wood where Jonty and I used to ride when we were a bit younger. It's a difficult ride, which made it kind of private. (Jont and I once saw a fox hiding there as the hunt went by on the path above – they couldn't reach it).' The ambulance man coughed. He wanted Chris to get on with it. 'I think Jonty wanted to take Holly there today. Unfortunately – ' here he grinned at me and the ambulance man – 'Holly's riding skills aren't up to it. But Tamara's are. I suspect she knew that Jonty would have to come and find her there without Holly.'

'Bit of an attention-seeker then, this young Tamara?'

'I'll say,' I said.

'I'll go looking,' Chris said. 'Give me a number to ring when I've got something to report.'

'We've got chaps in there looking,' said the man. 'But they didn't have much to go on. Your mate must have gone back in with both the horses. Unfortunately it's so muddy you can't tell which are the fresh hoof-marks.'

'Perhaps he hoped Skippy would lead him to Tamara.'

'I think she really loves that pony,' I said, thinking perhaps it was the only living creature that might return the affection.

The three of us crossed the road. I was going to station myself in the phone box where I could see up and down the road, into the pub car park and into the woods. We all exchanged phone numbers. I had a pocketful of coins and I felt quite important all of a sudden. Chris went off into the woods. Before today I hadn't even known he could ride, but I suppose it shouldn't have been a surprise. The ambulanceman went back into the car park to await instructions.

I stood in the phone box for a while. I was cold and damp and the rain drummed on the roof. Twenty minutes later nothing had happened, but the clouds had lifted a little and the rain had practically stopped. I wandered outside as far as I dared from the phone box and gazed into the woods. They were dripping and full of birdsong, but no clues as to where Tamara, then Jonty and now Chris had disappeared.

There were two huge conker trees at the beginning of the path. (Even I can recognise a conker tree at this time of year.) One or two early conkers had fallen on the ground. I stamped on one, out of habit, just to see the lovely shiny brown conker inside. There it was. I picked it up and leant against the tree. Then I saw our clue! Carved into the bark – the vandal! It was fresh. TH 4 J C-H. Well, that was pretty unambiguous! Perhaps she'd seen *As You Like It* too! Quite romantic as well, I had to admit. Perhaps the silly girl had done it on other trees and left a trail.

I nipped back into the phone box and rang Chris's mobile. It took a few rings before he answered. 'Hi Chris! Any news?'

'Nothing. It's very wet and slippery. Poor old Shakespeare is having to work hard.'

'I've got a clue, Chris.'

'What's that? Hey – hang on! I've just seen Jonty! *Jo-ont*!' he shrieked, deafening me on the end of the phone. 'Hol, I'll ring you back. I need two hands to gallop.'

I put the phone down. A few minutes later it rang. I grabbed it. 'Holly, hi. It's Jont.' He sounded flat and out of breath.

'No sign of her then?'

'Nope. Skippy doesn't seem to have a clue either. He just doesn't like rain and fluttering leaves much.'

'Are you going to your Foxhole place?'

'I think that's where she was heading, but she's not there, I've checked. Anyway, Chris said you had a "clue".'

'Well—' it was more embarrassing explaining it to Jonty. 'Just here at the entrance to the wood there's a tree with your and Tamara's initials carved into it. I wondered if she'd left a sort of trail. Didn't realise the silly cow was that stuck on you.'

'Huh. Neither did I. And I think we'll have a bit of an

embargo on nastiness about Tamara, Hol. She could be dead.'

Crikey. That made me feel terrible. 'Sorry,' I said in a small voice. 'Well, I hope the clue helps you to find her.' I put the phone down. Remorse was hitting me by the bucketload, even though she was horrible. I felt about two inches high. She tried to nick my boyfriend, dammit, why should I be all-forgiving? I slumped down onto the floor of the telephone box and waited.

About half an hour later there was a flurry of activity in the car park. A couple of police cars joined the ambulance and then they all drove away. A little later I could hear a helicopter circling. Perhaps they'd found her. I tried ringing Chris's mobile again, but all I got was a stupid woman telling me that the Vodaphone I was ringing was switched off. What was going on?

Half an hour after that I climbed on the bike and cycled back to Clermont Chase. There was still no one around. I went up to my room and had a long hot bath.

Eleven

I was warm and dry again at last. It was still pouring with rain outside, but I blow-dried my hair and put on a jersey for the first time this holiday. I was beginning to feel marooned in my room in an empty house yet again when I heard Flavia's Mini on the gravel and Jonty and her talking.

'She's even more stupid than Beatrice says she is,'

Flavia was saying. 'Idiotic to do a dangerous ride on your own without telling anyone where you're going. One of the first things you learn in Pony Club.'

They went out of earshot before I could hear Jonty's reply, but I was inclined to agree with Flavia. That was a first.

I wasn't sure how I was going to deal with Jonty – for all sorts of reasons – but curiosity got the better of me. I thought I could at least offer to make them some tea and toast. I went down to the kitchen. Jonty and Flavia were both by the Aga with their backs to me. Flavia was in fact putting the kettle on and Jonty was stripping off his wet clothes and hanging them over the rail. He was down to his boxer shorts when I walked in. 'Hi!' I said, to anyone who cared to listen.

Flavia of course didn't respond, but Jonty said, somewhat discouragingly and still with his back to me, 'Oh, Holly. It's you.'

'Well?' I said. 'What's happened? Did you find Tamara?'

Jonty turned around. I felt quite scared of him, even in his boxers with wet hair. 'I'm surprised you're interested,' he said, not looking me in the eye.

I could see he was exhausted. Last night's antics probably got him off to a bad start anyway. It was awful not knowing how much he'd been told about me and Chris. What if Chris had blurted it all out while they were riding together? Though I suppose I'd be flattering myself to imagine that I was their main topic of conversation just then. 'I was trying to help you find her,' I reminded him. 'I wasn't squatting in a damp telephone box in the middle of nowhere just for a laugh, you know.'

'OK, sorry,' said Jonty.

'I only want to know what happened. To you and Chris as well.'

'Let me get some clothes on and I'll tell you,' he said. But he still wasn't looking me in the eye. That was a very bad sign indeed.

'I've just made tea, Jonathan,' said Flavia to his departing footsteps.

'I'll be back in a sec – ' his voice floated down.

Flavia banged some crockery onto the table. I fetched cutlery. 'Ruined their lunch do,' said Flavia, not exactly *to* me, but at me. 'You can imagine – phone call from the hospital. Page-Joneses decided to go home.'

'So she's all right? Tamara's OK?'

'Depends what you call OK. I imagine what you call OK and I call OK aren't quite the same.'

Oh, very helpful, Flavia. 'I only asked,' I retorted, petulantly. I picked up a knife and put it down again. I seemed to have spent a lot of time in this vast house feeling trapped. Fortunately Jonty came in soon after that.

'That's better,' he said. 'I feel a bit more human now.' He poured himself a cup of tea.

'Can I have one?' I asked, desperate not to appear stand-offish. He poured me one and I loaded the sugar in again. Stirring it gave me something to do.

'OK,' Jonty began. 'Well, as soon as Mum said Tamara had gone missing I knew she'd have gone to the Foxhole. We were talking about it last night. I said I wanted to take you there and she asked if she could come. Thing is, it's too far to walk, and possibly too exciting a ride for you.'

'What do you mean?'

'Well – we hunt, so hedges and streams are all par for the course. I've done it for a couple of years now and

Tamara's been once, though Chris and I discovered the Foxhole when we were kids.'

'He told me. Anyway, never mind the whys and wherefores. Tell me about Tamara now.'

'OK. Well, she'd fallen off jumping a stream. You got it right about her leaving a trail of vandalised trees. We followed it and found her lying half in the water with her leg broken under her. We could see the bone sticking out. She kept passing out with pain. We called the ambulance people. They landed a helicopter as close as they could but it was still about a mile away. So they had to stretcher her to the helicopter and then airlift her to Birmingham. I'd left Skippy tied up so Chris and I had to ride Arnie and Shakespeare back to fetch him and then come back to the stables. The police wanted statements from us and then they drove us to the hospital.'

'The *police*?'

'Yes. The whole incident was pretty serious. They wanted background. All a bit embarrassing really.' He looked away. 'All that carving on trees. Somewhat unbalanced, our Tamara.'

'Yah!' said Flavia, her only contribution so far.

I found myself suppressing a smile. Oh, what had happened to Jonty's sense of humour. Wasn't it ever so slightly amusing, Tamara carving their initials on trees? Apparently not.

'I've never seen anyone in so much pain. We thought she was dead at first. She just looked like a bundle of bones, all muddy.'

'She is just a bundle of bones.' Jonty looked up at me fiercely. I cringed. 'I mean it. I – mean – I don't mean it unkindly. It's a fact.'

'It's all her own fault!' said Flavia. 'And if you're

anorexic your bones are bound to snap more easily. Oh well. She's certainly got the attention she wanted now.'

I saw Jonty's thunderous expression and decided to keep my mouth shut. Flavia left the kitchen just as Gina was coming in.

'Any news on the Hilton girl?' she asked cheerily. 'Oh, and Jonathan, you know you said you'd ride over to Granny's this evening don't you?'

'They found her,' I said. 'Jonty and Chris found her in the woods.'

'Was she all right?'

'No,' said Jonty dully, as if he didn't want to have to go through the whole thing again. 'She was badly injured. She's in hospital now.'

'Well,' said Gina, 'all's well that ends well. Why don't you two go and watch TV or something while I do supper? We should eat early tonight if you're going to Granny's, Jonathan. I'll drive you over if it's too unpleasant outside.'

'Shall we go and watch TV then?' I asked shyly. It was as if I didn't really know Jonty any more.

'Might as well,' he said, and shouldered his way through the door ahead of me.

We sat down without even turning the TV on.

'Please talk to me, Jonty,' I said. 'I can't bear this. I know a lot has happened, but most of it isn't my fault. It all started to go wrong with tickets to the ball.'

'And you made such a fuss. I'm used to it with my sisters, but not you, Holly.'

'Well, I'm sorry. But it's not my fault your grandmother fixed it for me to go with Chris, either. I had nothing to do with that.'

'Nor did Chris, poor guy. He loathes that sort of thing.'

(Hmmm. What had Chris told him then?) 'It was all a fiasco, as you probably heard, not least me being over-dressed in a ballgown.'

He smiled then. 'You looked gorgeous. 'Fraid I was too far gone to do you justice. I don't remember much after I saw you. Exhausted from giving Tamara a good time.'

'Jonty! What do you mean by that?'

'Well, poor kid.'

'She's the same age as us.'

'Yeah, but you wouldn't think it, would you?' He shook his head. 'It's just that everybody's horrible to her and then she makes it worse. I just wanted to be nice to her, see if it made any difference.'

I felt angry all over again. 'So where do you get off on that, Jonty Hayter? Because you saw what happened. She fell crash bang wallop in love with you – and then she only goes and tries to top herself!'

'She wasn't trying to *kill* herself. It was the old attention thing again.'

'So why did you do it? Isn't it enough having me in love with you?'

'Are you?' He narrowed his eyes at me – at least he was looking me in the eye.

But I hesitated, didn't I. 'Jont – one of the things I – like – about you, is the fact that you're so softhearted. But *her*! Why *her*?'

Now Jonty was cross again. 'You just don't get it, do you? You've met her mother and her sister. Her father isn't at home much, but she's bullied rotten at school. She told me some of the things the other girls do to her – not speaking to her for days, leaving her out of every-thing, hiding her underwear, her prep, her shoes. It's torture. And at home nobody listens to her either. They just spend money on her.'

'More than happens to me.'

'Holly! You know there's no comparison.'

I was stung. '*Anyway*,' I said, like a kid, 'you called her a stupid cow last night.'

'The less said about last night the better, I would have thought,' said Jonty coolly, (my gorgeousness clearly a thing of the past) standing up in response to a shout from Gina. 'But she is a stupid cow – for not realising what she's doing to herself.'

I trailed after Jonty into the kitchen. I hated myself. I hated this whole place for what it was doing to me – making me so jealous, so unsympathetic, and such a traitor.

Supper was rather a silent affair. Brian was away overnight apparently, so we didn't have him complimenting the chef all the time. It was something rather elaborate from M & S. Flavia was reading. Jonty told Gina in a bit more detail about the events of the day. Gina was very matter-of-fact about it all. 'Mother like that, hardly surprising,' sort of thing.

Flavia left the table with, 'Well, she succeeded in ruining her mother's day – and Beatrice's for that matter.'

I didn't say anything apart from 'Would you mind passing me the salad,' and 'Yes please' and 'Thank you'. It was raining again. Gina offered Jonty a lift to Dorothy's and went upstairs to change her shoes before leaving. I waited in the hall with Jonty. Clearly I wasn't invited to Dorothy's with him, but nobody gave any explanation. I tried to think of something positive to say about Tamara. I didn't want Jonty thinking I was a total bitch.

'Perhaps,' I ventured, 'It's a good thing Tamara's in hospital—'

I was going to say, so they can sort out her bulimia, but Jonty didn't give me time to finish. 'Oh yeah, so you don't have to be bothered with her before you leave!' he snapped. 'I'm used to that kind of snidey crap from Flavia, Holly, but not from you! There was me thinking you were kind-natured as well as strong-minded, but I was wrong, wasn't I?' We heard Gina coming down the stairs. 'We'll talk in the morning,' he said. 'Perhaps we should both sleep on it—' and he was gone.

Alone again. It was only seven o'clock. I thought of Dorothy and 'the whole evening ahead of us'. What sort of evening could I have? I certainly didn't want to spend it with Flavia. Or Gina. And I didn't particularly want to spend it with my diary again either. I sat in front of the TV for a bit. I like Friday-night TV – shows what a sad person I am. After a while I realised that I couldn't see the screen properly because the sun was reflected in it. I went to close the curtains and saw that the tattered clouds had pulled back on a spectacular evening. Everything was shining.

I had an idea. I went over to the phone in the corner of the room. (Phones in most rooms here.) After this morning I had the number of Chris's mobile off by heart. I dialled it. Uh-oh. 'The vodaphone you have called might be switched off . . .' Did I dare to ring the phone in his house? What if Jill answered? Perhaps I could offer to cycle Chris's bike back for him, since I had nothing else to do. That sounded normal didn't it? I fetched the number from where I'd pinned it by the kitchen phone and tried again.

Chris answered. Phew! 'Chris – could I come over? I'm on my own again – Jont's at Dorothy's – and I need to talk to someone.'

'Oh. OK then. I suppose. It's quite a long walk though.' He didn't sound that enthusiastic. 'Actually, you could do me a favour and cycle my bike back.' (He'd thought of it too.) 'It'll take you about twenty minutes. Mum's out collecting Toby, but I expect she could drive you home.'

'You sure?'

'Yes, why not.' (He was sounding keener now.) 'I'll tell you how to get here. Maybe you'd better write it down.'

I left a note saying that I was returning Chris's bike for him and that Jill would bring me back. I was kind of past caring what they all thought anyway, but I didn't think another runaway teenager was a good idea. I borrowed Jonty's cagoule from the rail on the Aga in case it rained again. I had to bounce the bike up and down a few times to shake the water off it. I swung my leg over the saddle, wobbled a bit and then set off, my backside instantly remembering the pain of it as I pedalled down the drive with Chris's instructions folded in the pocket of the cagoule.

It was a brilliant evening. The bike made a very satisfying swishing noise along the wet road. The birds were all singing and the sky was full of jazzy pink and gold vapour trails. It smelt fresh and rainwashed. I only met one car the whole way there, and that was a little old lady driving very slowly, thank goodness. The Greens' cottage stood alone. It fronted the road but a path led round to the back. I wheeled the bike round. No Deux Chevaux in sight. The cottage made an L-shape with a long, low wooden barn – Jill's studio I guessed. The outside walls were covered in climbing plants and the garden itself contained nothing but vegetables and herbs – and chickens. I could see lavender and marigolds between the marrows and tomato plants. The fields beyond stretched away to the west into a gentle valley. I leant the bike against the wall.

I knocked on the cottage door. I could hear Chris making his way downstairs. My heart was thumping in my chest. I hadn't quite thought this venture through. There had been so many unanswered questions and emotions flying around when I'd last been alone with Chris. Not to mention that kiss. I found myself remembering it as I stood there. The taste of his mouth. Where was he? I knocked on the door again and was surprised how quickly it opened.

'Did you knock before?' said Chris. 'I had some music on and then I came downstairs where the tumbledryer was making a racket. Still,' he beamed, 'at least I've got some dry clothes to wear.' He ducked outside the low front door and stood facing me. He had bare feet under his loose jeans and a top that had obviously just been pulled from the dryer. I could smell its warm, pleasantly synthetic scent from where I stood. His hair was still damp from being washed and towelled dry. I could see traces of the famous curls. And the big dark eyes with the sunset shining in them. Orlando. I did a naughty thing. I reached up and pulled his head down to kiss me. I hadn't planned it. It was just that he was irresistible in that tousled state.

After a while he pulled back and wiped his mouth with the back of his hand. 'I don't think we should stand here. I don't know when Mum and Tobes will turn up. Come indoors.' I followed him into the cottage.

My first impression was that it smelt lovely – of beeswax and woodsmoke and flowers, with slight laundry and shower smells in the background. Chris turned, ducking again under the low lintel into a sitting room where a sofa covered in a Welsh blanket faced a log fire. 'Mum lit it when I came in soaked,' he said. 'Do you want to take that cagoule off indoors?'

I pulled it off over my head, trying not to take my T-shirt off with it. Mistake. I should have remembered Chris's reactions to bare flesh. It was like the starter's gun had gone off. My arms were still tangled in the cagoule when he pulled it off for me and held me in a clinch before I could fight back – if I'd wanted to. We kind of subsided on to the sofa. This wasn't like cuddling up in front of the TV with Jonty. This was more like – a – match, a championship match. Huh, a love match. Jonty was laid back and casual, fluid and smooth, but Chris gave it all he'd got. Not that I was really comparing them, you understand. Our T-shirts were getting rucked up when Chris sat up suddenly and listened. I heard it too. Jill was back. 'Come into the kitchen,' he said. 'I'll make some coffee and tell Mum why you're here. You don't need to go back straight away do you?'

I laughed ruefully. 'I actually came here to talk, Chris. True to form, we've hardly spoken a word yet!'

He gave me a sort of smiling frown. 'And of course, you brought my bike back. I just don't want Mum muscling in on you. I'll tell her I'm giving you a tour of the studio. She'll leave us alone then. She hates showing off her work. And I know Toby wants to watch something on TV.' He hauled me into the kitchen just before Jill and Toby came in the door.

'Ooh, I didn't know we were expecting company,' said Jill. 'Hello, Holly.'

'Holly brought my bike back,' said Chris. 'They've all deserted her at the Chase.'

'No manners, have they, these aristos,' said Jill,

hanging up her coat. 'Only joking. I'd forgotten Dorothy was expecting Jonty tonight. She likes to have the kids on their own. She and Jonty play chess on Fridays when he's at home.'

'I thought I'd show Holly the studio while she's here.'

'Fine, fine,' said Jill. 'I haven't eaten yet, so I'll fix myself some food and perhaps we'll have coffee together later?'

Chris hustled me off. There was a way into the studio through a bolted door. The door rattled and squeaked back and we were faced with this huge barn area, the bare walls painted white and hung with more of Jill's paintings. I was struck again by how beautiful they were, but quite frankly, if you've just got off with a boy, you don't *really* want to find yourself looking at enormous paintings of female bottoms and breasts with him. Chris is used to the paintings, of course, but I'm not. He had his arm round my waist and ran his hand up and down the side of my body, tweaking under my T-shirt as he passed the gap. 'Your skin is so *warm*,' he whispered.

'Chris!' I barked. 'Just show me the paintings, and then I want to talk.'

'You sure?' he said, right into my ear. I could feel his breath. 'Do we have to talk?'

We'd reached the end of the barn. There was a separate section here as if someone else used it. Well, someone else must have used it, because the art was quite different. The pieces were mostly 3-D, some made in metal, others in strange rusty fabric pulled taut over wire frames. There were a few paintings – they were abstracts in purples and bronzes, full of movement. My eye was caught by an unfinished painting on the easel – a flash of bright pink and bronzey black. The top of the black was dotted with more bright pink in flower shapes.

The whole thing was vivid with life and energy, like someone dancing. The colours were very different from Jill's but there was the same strength and confidence.

'Does your mum share this studio with another artist, then?' I asked, trying to ignore his hand resting on my hip.

'In a manner of speaking, yes, she does.'

'And what's that supposed to mean, Christopher Green?' I asked, smiling at the rhyme.

'It depends whether you describe the other person's work as art or not.'

'I think it's fabulous. Of course, I like your mum's work too,' I said, not wanting to offend him. 'Do Gina and Dorothy buy and sell the other artist's stuff too?'

Chris actually let go of me for half a second and laughed out loud. 'It's *my* stuff, Holly! GCSE work!'

'Wow. It's brilliant.' I was silenced. I suppose you might expect an artist's son to be an artist too. I just didn't expect a silent fifteen-year-old tennis player to be one.

'Good art department at my school,' he said modestly. 'Honestly. It makes Mum laugh seeing people pay out for private education when there's an art department like ours on their doorstep. It's one of the best in the country. Good for sport too, so that's me covered.'

'What do you want to do later?' I asked.

'Dunno. What about you?'

'Dunno either. English at university probably. My school's really good on English. And history.'

'Hol, do you still want to talk – or can we go and find Mum's studio couch?'

'I do want to talk. About Jonty and Tamara and stuff. Jonty's terribly angry with me and I want to know how much he knows about last night.'

'Ah. Perhaps we'd better find Mum's studio couch anyway.' We sat down a little way apart from each other. 'OK. As I see it, Jonty takes Tamara to dance so she can show off new designer dress. Jonty would prefer to take girlfriend, but no big deal, he knows she's well taken care of by the extraordinary Dorothy. Jont, being Jont and a big softie, is nice to Tamara because it comes more easily to him than being nasty. Tamara, who has never had anyone be nice to her, as far as I can tell, reacts like an ill-treated stray dog and latches on to him bigtime. Jont finds it a bit of a strain, especially as she keeps eating and then running off to the loo to make herself sick. In fact he finds it rather distressing and turns to the vile wine to pass the time while she's off in the Ladies. Surprise entrance of Christopher and Holly, Holly looking particularly stunning. Tamara is devastated. Jonty doesn't know how to handle the situation and is too far gone to do much about it anyway. (Jonty told me all this this morning – I got it wrong too.) Now, this is the tricky part, and I haven't been entirely truthful with Jonty about it. When Tamara saw us together, she flipped. Jonty had just turned on her because he couldn't handle both of you, remember? (Though the poor girl had looked after him while he threw up anyway.) Because then she saw that you – the girl he spurned *her* for – couldn't care all that much about *him*.'

I didn't like this at all. 'Oh dear. So she ran away?'

'Not sure when. She went home with her sister and changed, but they think she slept in their stables. Skippy's the only one who understands her, sort of thing. By the way, Beatrice told Flavia about us. Flavia probably couldn't care less but she did mention it to Jonty in a vague sort of way. So when Jonty asked me about it – challenged me about it – I said I was keeping you warm or something corny like that.'

'You *were* keeping me warm. That wasn't a lie.'

'But I told him you didn't mean anything to me, and that *was* a lie.'

He gave me a puppy-dog look and was about to lunge at me again, but I stopped him. There was more I needed to know. 'So Jonty isn't angry with me because of you?'

'Don't think so. But searching for Tamara today was really distressing, really traumatic, especially for Jonty. I'm sort of over it now I've been home and – and you're here. We thought she was dead. She just looked like this little crumpled heap of bones, all muddy—'

'That's what Jonty said.'

'It was scary. I called the ambulance people straight away, so at least I had something to do, but Jont slid down the bank to check whether or not she was still breathing. Her bone was sticking out through the mud. It was horrible – like those pictures you see of corpses in the trenches, in the First World War. She kept coming round and whimpering and then fainting again. It seemed ages until the medics arrived. And then it was awful watching them get her on to the stretcher, though they'd given her something by then. Jont kept saying, "Poor kid – this is all my fault." Actually I kind of suspected it might be all our faults, but I kept quiet about that.'

'Ultimately it's her family's fault, Chris, not yours or mine or Jonty's. Sending her away to a school she hates. Buying her off with designer dresses instead of affection. Food as power. But I'm beginning to see why Jonty was so angry with me. I've been horrible about Tamara. Actually, I think he's cross with himself too, for letting Flavia bully him into taking Tamara to the dance last night. After all, none of this would have happened if he'd taken me.'

Chris leant over and rubbed his face against mine. 'But then none of this would have happened either, would it?' He kissed me. 'We'd better go. Otherwise Mum might stalk up on us and catch us all unawares, and that would be embarrassing.'

'Can we look at your paintings again, now I know who the artist is?'

'OK.'

I stopped in front of the easel. 'Is this a GCSE one?'

'You know it isn't.'

'So when did you paint it?'

'Earlier on.'

'It's me, isn't it?'

'Of course it's you.' He looked down at me with melty eyes. 'You are the only image I have in my head right now.' He touched my forehead with his lips and we went off to find Jill.

Jill was watching TV with Toby. They were very engrossed. She looked up with a start. 'Oh, Holly, I said I'd give you a lift back didn't I? Would you awfully mind waiting until this is over? It's quite long I'm afraid.'

'Ssshhh, Mum!' Toby admonished.

'It's OK, Mum,' said Chris. 'We'll walk back. It's still a nice evening. I'll wheel my bike. See you later.'

'Bye Jill,' I whispered.

Twelve

Friday night

I've just walked back across the fields with Chris (and his bike). It was the most romantic walk I've ever had in my life. The sky was still rosy and the stars were popping out. And then a huge moon came up, all golden and strange. No one was around, we were completely alone. We kept stopping to kiss and Chris told me over and over again that he was crazy about me. He is so sexy. I can't think how I didn't see it at first. It's partly his eyes. He never looked me in the eye at the beginning of the week. And his sinewy strength. We jumped over straw bales and rode around on his bike together like kids. We lay down and hugged and rolled down a slope still hugging, over and over.

But now the awful bit. He said goodbye before we got here because we didn't want to bump into Jonty. And it was really goodbye. He's going to a tennis tournament somewhere tomorrow – all weekend. So I might never see him again. It's over. How could we carry on? We both cried. I'm crying now as I write. I can't bear it. He said that I had to do what I wanted, but that he would never tell Jonty. Their friendship goes back for ever and it means a lot to them both. So of course I won't tell him either. Chris thinks Jonty won't be angry with me about Tamara any more tomorrow. Says he never stays angry for long. He (Chris) understood my feelings about privilege too, though he says that he and I are every bit as privileged, far more than Tamara. I know what he's saying, but he's grown up with the lords of the manor, people with just so much more money. I haven't. My parents are old lefties. Jill probably is too, but maybe she's had to put her politics on one side a bit.

Tomorrow is the last day of this strange holiday. Tomorrow I will pretend Chris never happened and concentrate on me and Jonty, who is, when all is said and done, a sweetheart.

Oh yes. And Chris does know Joel, one of Alex's brothers – in fact he'll be in the tournament tomorrow. Small world, huh?

I don't know how I slept. I kept wanting to get up and run across the fields to Chris's. I wanted us to be together all his last night, not apart. When I woke up it was bright outside.

I sat up in bed for a bit of positive thinking. Today was my last day. I wanted to stay friends with Jonty. I certainly didn't want him thinking so badly of me. I hopped over to the mirror and looked at myself hard. Actually, I didn't altogether like what I saw. Holly Davies. Slag. Comes to Clermont Chase to stay with Jonty, my holiday romance. And gets off with his best friend. Not to mention being rude to his family and unkind about a girl with a serious eating disorder, simply because she happened to fancy my boyfriend. Jont knew Chris fancied me, but he didn't let it bother him, did he? Because he trusted me. And I'd betrayed that trust. And Dilly's trust too. *Don't mess with Chris.*

I had a shower and washed away some of the self disgust. Jonty's family *were* pretty difficult to deal with. Tamara *was* a pain. Chris had fallen in love with *me*. It might sound trivial to blame it all on the ball tickets, but I had been seriously disappointed. Really it boiled down to our different values. Meals out, expensive theatre seats, ballgowns – Davieses and Hayter-Clermonts put different values on them. Where Greens stood in all this I don't know. There was Jill, hugely talented, struggling and juggling with flower-arranging and cleaning to keep her family afloat while Clermonts see her art as a valuable *investment*. It's all a mystery to me.

I tried to extract what was important here. Jonty-and-Chris was important. They understood one another. Were friends without jealousy. I didn't want to leave scars on that friendship. My self-esteem was important too. I wanted the Hayters to rate me – I didn't want to give them any reason to feel superior. OK, we weren't rich, but I was every bit as good as them.

So. Today. Today I had to make my peace with Jont. No Chris or Tamara to get in the way. It was half-past ten. *Again!* Time to get started.

'Morning Holly.' Brian.

'Hello dear. Sleep well?' Gina.

Silence. Flavia.

'Hi Hol.' Jonty. At least he was speaking to me.

'So what's on the cards for my last day?'

'Granny. She wants to take you and me on a picnic to Charlcote. Her house at 12.30. Which gives us an hour or so to go on the quad bikes.'

'Quad bikes! You've got quad bikes?'

'Yeah, well, we got them a couple of years ago so the excitement's worn off a bit. Granny reminded me that you might enjoy them.'

'Wow!'

'They're in the garage. But they won't run away while we have some breakfast. I've only just got up. Didn't fancy riding this morning somehow.'

'Well don't expect me to come,' said Flavia.

Jonty flashed me a grin. As if. 'It's OK Flaves. We can manage.' Perhaps he'd had a bit of a think too. And Chris said he never stayed angry for long.

We walked over to the garage. We didn't hold hands or anything. Jonty shot me sidelong glances.

'I'm really sorry—'

'I'm really sorry—'

We both spoke at once. 'Me first,' said Jonty. 'I'm sorry I gave you such a hard time about Tamara. It was just seeing her like that, thinking she was dead and that it was my fault for treating her as badly as everyone else.'

'Wasn't your fault, Jonty.' I came *very* close to saying it was mine. But then I stopped myself. It wasn't my fault either. As I'd said to Chris, the problem went far deeper than that. 'I'm sorry I was so mean about her. Guess I felt kind of insecure.'

'Friends?' he said, holding out his hand.

'Friends,' I said, and took it.

I wish I'd known about the bikes before. Now *they* are rich people's toys I can really get to grips with. I've always wanted to have a go. Jonty and I put on the helmets and tore noisily across their land with no one to irritate. It was fast and smelly and exhilarating, just what we needed. We careered round like kids, delinquent kids. And when we finally got off them, our whole bodies vibrating and our ears ringing, Jont was full of admiration. 'Can't believe you've never done that before, Holly! You were wicked at it.'

Well, I thought, it's not like tennis or riding – you don't need years of practice. Just energy and a sense of fun. We peeled off the helmets and overalls. 'I'll miss you,' said Jonty.

'I'll miss you too,' I said truthfully.

Dorothy drove a small Mercedes people-carrier. It suited her somehow. Our picnic had been ordered from the local delicatessen and packed into a number of coolbags.

Hey, this was stylish. The day had started grey but now it was beginning to brighten up. 'This is good,' said Dorothy. 'It means that most of the tourists will have chosen to go somewhere indoors.' I thought it was quite strange to be visiting a country house for a picnic when you had an entire grockle-free estate of your own, but Dorothy seemed keen on the idea of a day out. She pulled into a parking space under the trees and gave us each a rug and a coolbag to carry. 'Now, isn't this fun?' she asked us. 'I'd have ended up watching the cricket on television if I'd stayed at home. Much better to sit by the river and watch the deer. You might like to go round the house together after lunch while I take a nap, but it's not obligatory.'

Over lunch Dorothy asked us both about yesterday.

'Didn't Jonty tell you last night?' I asked.

'No dear. Jonathan didn't want to talk about it last night – did you Jon?' (Jon, that sounded more grown-up than Jonty.) 'Anyway, we had a chess championship to concentrate on.'

I began, 'Well, the first I heard of it, Gina knocked on my door at about nine in the morning and said that they'd heard from the Hiltons. No one seemed very worried at that point. My parents would have been frantic.'

'Mother woke me up a bit after that.' Jonty joined in. 'Tamara'd been telling me at the polo-club bash about how she didn't want to go back to school next term – in between dashing off to make herself throw up. She kept saying, "No one will listen to me." I guess that's the main problem.'

'Imagine,' I said, 'having to go away from home to a place where people bully you mercilessly. Why do they make her go?'

'No imagination!' said Dorothy. 'They can't imagine what it's like for her.'

'Well I can,' said Jonty. 'Remember my awful prep school, Granny?'

'Of course I do, dear. Your poor mother was desperate. I had to insist she took you away.'

'Thank goodness you did.'

I'd forgotten that Jonty'd had a taste of what Tamara was going through. And I suppose even I had had a taste of homesickness this week. Maybe I should have used my imagination a bit more on Tamara.

'She doesn't help herself, though,' said Jonty. 'In fact she's not very bright, not even very likeable. She's only interested in clothes – and her pony, of course.'

'Jonty—'

'You're quite right about her, Holly. She's a complete pain in the neck. She just doesn't deserve to feel so lonely. Do you know, Granny, when we first found her, and thought she was dead, I was almost glad for her. I thought at least she wasn't miserable any more. Still. Maybe she'll get the attention she needs now.'

'The doctors are bound to see that she's anorexic and try to do something about that,' said Dorothy. 'And she might have got her wish about not going back to school.'

'That's the thing about wishes, isn't it?' I said.

'What is?' said Jonty.

'You know, like I said—' but then I stopped, because it was Chris I'd said that to.

'I heard that helicopter,' said Dorothy. 'I wondered what was going on. Of course, Holly had rung me, so I knew something was up.'

'You rang Granny?' Jonty asked. I realised there were lots of things he didn't know.

'I had to start somewhere. You just told me to get help. I didn't know where to begin. I didn't know anyone's names, let alone their phone numbers.'

Jonty sat back and looked at me with something like respect. 'I really do owe you an apology, Hol. You know, I forgot all that part. You must have organised the emergency services and Chris and everything.'

Dorothy poured herself a large glass of wine and regarded us with a half smile on her face.

'Well, I was impressed by the fact that you'd just gone out there.'

'It seems that Tamara has quite a lot to thank you both for,' said Dorothy. 'Now, run along you two. I fancy a little nap in the sun, and I don't want to have to listen to you apologising to each other all afternoon.'

Jonty stood up. 'Oh all right, Granny. Back in an hour, OK?'

'That's fine dear,' she said, and leant back against a tree with her newspaper.

'Come on, Hol,' he said, pulling me to my feet. We set off holding hands. I had the distinct feeling that this was the precise scenario Dorothy'd had in mind.

We wandered up to the house. 'Do you want to go in?' Jonty asked.

'Not particularly,' I said. 'It's nice just wandering here by the river. Gosh, imagine owning all of this.'

'I don't have to imagine,' Jonty said, and I felt foolish. 'Holly, I can't *help* who I am, or what I was born into, you know.'

I looked at him standing by the river. He was wearing baggy trousers and a T-shirt – a boy like any other – but then my brain conjured up a strange vision of ten or fifteen Jon Clermonts going back for centuries: lanky young men with a flop of hair and a ready smile, and a look in their eyes that told you how secure they were in their lineage, both past and future. I imagined them standing there, in tabards and ruffs and cloaks and Edwardian suits. I tried to imagine being Jonty, tried to imagine living in a house and grounds that generations of my family had owned. I know that families like Jont's are rare these days – they have to find other ways of keeping the estate going, like Gina and her art buying. But it's just a different world.

'Hey!' he snapped his fingers in front of my face. 'Where've you been? You went off into a daze just then!'

'Nowhere,' I said. 'Right here.'

'It's changed, hasn't it?' he said wistfully.

'I suppose it has.'

'You fight against me Holly. You fight against my family and the system I live in. I want you to relax and enjoy it, but you can't quite, can you?'

'I do want to, Jont. I try to imagine living your life, I do, but you have to imagine mine, too.'

'I'd love your life. Nice normal parents. Friends living in the road. School round the corner. Comfortable with people up and down the social scale. My life will improve when I get a car and I'm allowed to use the London flat, but until then I have to make do with the Christophers and Tamaras of this world.'

'Nothing wrong with Chris!' I felt he needed defending.

'You said it!' Jonty laughed, and I wondered again how much he knew. 'Chris is the one who keeps me in touch with the real world. Actually, Jill's probably the one who keeps me in touch with the real world. She does the same for Mum. And Granny.'

'I love Dorothy.'

'Well lucky old Granny. You don't love me any more, do you?'

'Jonty!'

'I'm not bitter about it. I just know it's not how it was in Barbados.'

'Jont—'

'Yes?'

'Can I say that I love you for being my first boyfriend?'

'Gee, thanks.'

'No, I mean it. I'll never have another first boyfriend.'

'You mean, I can't be the first and only?'

'No,' I said, too quickly and too definitely.

He gave me a long, cool look. 'I'm not going to ask, Holly, because I don't want to know. I want it to be like it was before, but I know it can't be.' Then he leant over and gave me the tenderest of kisses.

'Hold my hand,' I said, as we walked along the river path. 'For old times' sake?'

He held it. 'So as not to disappoint Granny,' he said.

So that's how a relationship ends.

When we got back Dilly was there in the kitchen.

'Hi Holly! I couldn't be bothered to wait until tomorrow to come home. Seemed crazy to miss you. You don't mind sharing her do you, little bro?'

'What can I say?' said Jonty gallantly. He ruffled my hair. 'I promised I'd play tennis with Toby tonight anyway.'

'Chris not here?' asked Dilly.

'No,' I said, 'he's playing in a weekend tournament, somewhere in Hertfordshire I think.'

'More than I knew,' said Jonty. But he was laughing. I

think we were both glad Dilly was home. Jonty disappeared off to change.

Dilly got two cokes out of the fridge and handed me one. We sat down at the kitchen table. 'So. What's it been like? You and Jonty still like this?' She linked her little fingers.

'Pretty good,' I said non-committally. 'This place is really beautiful.'

'Pity the pool's out of action,' said Dilly. 'Only thing that makes it bearable in hot weather. Can't think what you've found to *do* here. Still, won't ask.'

'We swam at Bury,' I said. Then, 'I suppose you've heard the Tamara saga?'

'Nothing but,' said Dilly. 'Silly idiot. Fancy going off in conditions like that without even leaving a note. She's not even much of a rider.'

'Better than me,' I said. 'Though that's not hard!'

'I thought you rode.'

'Pony trekking riding. Not like you lot. I panic if the horse so much as canters!'

'Good job you're not here in the hunting season then,' said Dilly.

I kept quiet this time.

Saturday night

My last night. This time tomorrow I'll be in my own little bed, and I can't wait. Can't wait to see Alex and Zoe and Josie and Mum and Dad and Abby. Didn't think it was possible to miss them so much.

It was great seeing Dilly, especially as Jonty and I have basically broken up. Of course she wanted to know what I thought of everything. She kept saying 'So what did you think of blah?' – Chris/Bury/Stratford/everything. I answered carefully. She so much wanted me to love it all. Which of course is what Jonty wanted me to do too. Oh well.

Chris, where are you now? Staying with a tennis person in St Albans, but I can't picture it. Are you thinking about me as much as I'm thinking about you? I must contact Alex as soon as I get home and get a message to you through her brother.

Tomorrow this will all seem like a dream, a play.

Thirteen

Dilly came crashing into my room at 8.30. 'Get up Holly. Come down and have breakfast with me.'

'Uh? What's the time? It's too early!'

'No it's not. Jont went out hours ago.'

'Hours?'

'An hour and a half.'

'So he's on a horse again. I thought the hunt for Tamara had put him off.'

'Jont? Nah. There's this new horse that he really likes. But he wanted to be back to take you to the coach station. Thought I'd pass on that one myself.'

'Any news on Tamara?' I got out of bed and went into the shower. Dilly carried on talking.

'Flavia says they're keeping her in. Horrible old Beatrice can't see what all the fuss is about. Their dad has actually come home from Bahrain or somewhere to see Tamara.'

'Good.'

'What do you care?'

'Well, perhaps all that attention-seeking actually means she needs some attention.'

'True. Hurry up in there. I'm used to eating at 8 o'clock sharp on the course. I'm starving!'

'Go on down then. Mine's an orange juice!' She went. How much easier the week would have been in some ways with Dilly here. Then again, she wouldn't have let me near Chris!

Jont and Dilly were already troughing away when I got downstairs. The table was littered with cereal packets and yoghurt pots and juice cartons. More evidence of Dilly being at home. 'Pity you're off today, Holly. I was just thinking, I could have given you some proper riding lessons. Then, next time you stay, you could follow the hunt with us.'

Jonty was looking at me to see what I would say. 'I'd love to be able to ride better,' I said cautiously. 'Jont and I never got our picnic at Foxhole, did we? And I can't put all the blame on Tamara.'

'No,' said Jonty, equally cautiously, 'we can't put all the blame on Tamara.'

'So?' said Dilly. 'We've got, what, two hours. What shall we do? At least come and say hello to the horses. Tell you what, I'll put you on Gorse on a lead rein and we could all ride over to Granny's. What do you think Jont?'

'Don't mind,' said Jonty. 'What do you think Holly?'

'I think I'd feel safe enough. I'd better change though.'

Dilly helped me up onto Gorse. I felt so high above the ground. 'Go slowly, won't you?' I pleaded. Jonty went on ahead on Shakespeare and Dilly led me on Blue-bottle.

'We'll just walk,' she said. 'Gorse will follow Blue-bottle. They're great friends.'

'Do horses have friends?'

'Course they do.'

By the time we came to dismount at Dorothy's I was mighty proud of myself. Jonty was already in there eating chocolate Hobnobs. 'Granny!' shrieked Dilly.

'Cordelia, darling.' Dorothy hugged her warmly. 'How lovely to have you home. And what fun to have you two girls together! You will come again, won't you Holly? Do you know, Cordelia, I had to play fairy godmother to your friend here, and send her to the ball?'

Jonty looked at his watch. 'We haven't got long, Granny. You'll have to gossip another time.'

'Jonathan! I don't gossip!'

'No, of course you don't, Granny. But Holly's coach won't wait, and we've got to get her back in one piece on Gorse before we can even drive to the coach station.'

'All right my dears,' said Dorothy. She came over to me and gave me a hug too. 'Goodbye Holly. I've so enjoyed meeting you.'

'Not half as much as I've enjoyed meeting you,' I said. 'It's been great having a fairy godmother!'

'Even if my spells didn't always quite work out as intended, eh?' Dorothy chuckled to herself, and waved us off to the horses.

'What was all that about spells?' Dilly asked.

'Oh, just Granny being daffy as usual,' said Jonty.

Gina drove us to the coach station in the Range Rover. The coach station was concrete and tawdry and smelly. It was crowded with the old and the poor, people with carrier bags and clapped out old buggies and too many children. Gina gave me a brief hug. 'Goodbye Gina,' I said. 'Thank you so much for having me, and taking me to the theatre and everything.'

'Goodbye dear, come again,' she said in return, but I could see that already she was vague about me. How long before she'd find it hard to remember which one was Holly? She got back into the car and made herself comfortable with the Sunday papers.

Jonty carried my case. I was anxious about finding the right coach and getting a seat. I've led a sheltered life – it was my first long journey alone. Jonty checked all the numbers on the coaches, the bus stops and my ticket for me, and we found the one to London eventually. 'We make a good team,' I joked.

'Yeah,' he said. 'I think we met too young. I mean – this is husband and wife stuff. We'd be good at that wouldn't we?'

'Yup. Couple of little kids in tow.'

'Charlie and Georgina!'

'Sam and Ellie more like!'

'And we'd give them all the attention they wanted, wouldn't we?'

We looked at each other, not knowing whether to carry on laughing or start crying. Jont put my case down and threw his arms round me. Big, huggy squeeze. We straightened up. 'OK,' he said, 'here's the deal. In seven years time, to the day, to the minute – it's 12 noon – we'll meet at – at—'

'Somewhere that's neutral territory – that'll still be standing. I know, on the steps of the National Gallery!'

'Done,' he said, and slapped my hand.

We handed over my case to be loaded into the boot of the coach. 'I can write, can't I?'

'E-mail, perhaps. All students have it.'

'We might end up at the same university,' I said, climbing into the coach.

'That would be the best!' called Jonty.

'Bye! Thanks for having me!'

'Bye! Thanks for coming!' And he ran off, his flickering stride a joy to watch.

As our tatty coach revved up for the journey to London I saw the sleek Range Rover pulling away, heading back down the leafy lanes to Clermont Chase.

Epilogue

Ah, the bliss of being home again! Mum, Dad and Abby were all there to meet me at the coach station. We had homemade lentil lasagne – which I love – for supper. My bedroom seemed tiny but so much my own. Abby and Dad wanted to know everything, but Mum, bless her, was all for me having a long bath and getting a good night's sleep first.

I woke up with a cold. Odd to have one in the summer, but Mum thought it might have something to do with getting wet and hanging out in damp phone boxes.

Anyway, I was better by the time we started planning our end-of-holiday sleepover. Strangely enough, Alex and Zoe were both vying to have it. 'We're having it at Zoe's,' Alex said when she rang. 'But only because she's got more room.'

'Fine,' I said. 'I'm surprised you ever wanted it at your house. You usually can't wait to get out.'

'Ah, well I might just have a lot to tell you,' she said. 'But not a word until Sunday night, OK? It's not fair if we all tell each other everything before Josie gets back.'

Zoe rang to confirm. 'My place,' she said. 'I've got loads to tell you all. What about you, Holly? Oh no, I can't ask yet can I? Can't wait for Sunday!'

The rest of the week passed with buying shoes and stationery, a visit from my little cousins, taking Abby to the cinema. I sensed the summer ebbing away. Maddy called. It felt funny telling her that my Barbados romance hadn't lasted but she was very matter-of-fact about it. 'Can't last, can it?' she said. 'You're in different places.'

'But that wouldn't matter if we really loved each other, would it?' I was actually thinking about Chris.

'Course it would,' she said. 'You can't stay a nun, can you? We're too young to get serious about anyone. There are far too many exciting new people to meet.' I wasn't so sure. I missed Chris like hell. But then I'd missed Jonty before. Maybe I'd have to talk to the others about this.

Josie rang at last on the Saturday night. It was late, after eleven. I snatched up the phone – I'd been expecting her to call since six. She was all squeaky. 'Hey, Holly, you'll never guess what . . .' (but no lisp). I persuaded her to save it for tomorrow night – partly because I wanted a little more time to think about my week in the country before opening it up for inspection and comment from the others.

We all turned up amazingly punctually at Zoe's. Because her mum's American they have a huge freezer jampacked with food. We had burgers and chips and salad, with Haagen Daz – about five different flavours – for afters. Zoe practically has her own flat in their basement. They used to let it out, but now it's Zoe's and it's brilliant. 'OK, who's going first?' said Zoe.

'Me!' said Alex and Josie simultaneously.

'Let's go in alphabetical order,' said Zoe. 'That'll put me last, which suits me fine, but I don't think Alex is going to be able to hold out much longer.'

'This is all such a surprise,' said Alex. 'First of all I want to thank my agent, and my two cats, and of course the weird guy in the cyber-café, without whom . . .'

'Get on with it!' shouted Josie.

'Well guys, you have to remember that this is all very new and exciting for me . . .' Alex was away. Seems like the last couple of weeks have been a bit of a steep learning curve in the ways of womanhood for her.

I was next. Trouble was, as I recounted my story I realised that I came out of it all rather poorly, my pique over not being invited to the ball seemed so petty compared with Tamara's misfortunes. And as for getting off with Jonty's best friend . . .

But then Alex butted in. 'Is there any chance that your tennis-playing Chris Green was in Hertfordshire last weekend, and that he is in fact the same tennis-playing Chris Green that my brother Joel knows?'

'Why yes! Of course! I knew there was a connection! I completely forgot to ask you. I'd meant to try and get a message to him through you, until I realised that it would have been too late.'

'You know of course that this puts a completely different complexion on things, don't you?' said Alex gravely.

'Why?'

'Because Joel's tennis-playing Chris Green is gorgeous. Quiet. Smouldering eyes. With dark curly hair. I haven't seen him since last year, but I liked him then, even before I understood what you lot saw in boys.'

'No curls now,' I said. 'Shaved head, practically.'

'I wasn't talking about his head,' said Alex.

'Oh shut up.'

'Go on Josie,' said Zoe, 'Your turn.' Josie arranged herself comfortably, settling in for a long story (while Alex muttered in the background, 'his armpits, naturellement').

Josie's story was just as complicated as mine, if not more so. She didn't see it herself, but I reckon she came out of it even worse than I did. She did recognise that best friend's *boyfriend (as opposed to best friend's girlfriend) is a complete no-no. But she said it wasn't quite like that.*

As for Zoe. Well, true to form, Zoe's week doing Community Theatre had had a profound effect on her. No straightforward fluffy romance for her. Hers had encompassed race and culture and, well, Life, really. Still, mine had raised questions of class, and attitudes, among others.

. . . And my few hours with Chris. If they weren't true romance, then I don't know what is.

Also in the *GIRLS LIKE YOU SERIES:*

Sophie

Blonde, drop-dead beautiful Sophie is used to getting her own way, and not worrying about the broken hearts she leaves behind. She's determined that a family camping holiday in France is not going to cramp her style. What's more she knows exactly who she wants . . . but does he feel the same way about her?

Hannah

Hannah is the clever one, and hard to please – but she's really shy too. She doesn't fancy her chances on a summer music course – so she decides that the boys are just not worth bothering about . . . not any of them . . . or are they?

Charlotte

Shy, dreamy Charlotte has been going to the Lake District every year for as long as she can remember and she's loved Josh from afar for as long. But this year she's going without her older sister. It might be the chance she's been waiting for. What if Josh notices her – just because she's four years younger than him – it doesn't mean all her dreams won't come true – does it?

Maddy

Finding romance has never been a problem for Maddy – she's always been a beauty and dramatic with it. So she can't wait for her exotic holiday in Barbados with Dad – it's going to be brilliant, and so different from life at home with impoverished Mum. The stage is set – but is romance all that lies in store for Maddy?

Alex

With four brothers at home, Alex has always been one of the lads. Not for her all this starry-eyed romance stuff. Every summer she plays in a tennis tournament. This year it's the under 16s – and mixed doubles partners really matter. Suddenly Alex finds it's not her tennis technique she's concentrating on – and she's more determined than ever to win a different sort of match.

Josie

Sun, sea and sand: a perfect setting for a holiday romance and Josie's off to a Cornish beach to find one. She's been spending her summers there since – well . . . forever, and this year she's determined to be Queen of the Scene in the popularity stakes, even if it means trying to pull her best friend's boyfriend! It's bound to end in tears for one of them – but who?

Zoe

The last thing smart, beautiful Zoe wanted to spend the last precious days of her summer holiday doing was taking her little brother to the local Community Theatre Project. But waiting in the wings is the mysterious, exciting, unpredictable Lennie, and Zoe is swept off her feet by him and his passion for the Project. If only he could burn with the same passion for her. Zoe decides to make it happen – but the results aren't quite what she expected!